A New Beginning

Book 1 in the Blended Blessings Series

by

CaSandra McLaughlin & Michelle Stimpson

UF
McLaughl

Scriptures quotations from King James Version unless otherwise noted.
Cover by The Killion Group - www.TheKillionGroupInc.com
Edited by Karen McCollum Rodgers -
www.CritiqueYourBook.com

Acknowledgments from CaSandra McLaughlin

Praise God from whom all blessings flow, it's in Him that I live, move and have my being. I am who I am because of who He is, so I give God all the praise because this wouldn't be possible without Him.

I want to thank my parents, Cozella Miles, J.D. and Hazel Marshall for all of their love and support. Love to my grandparents, Ann Beckham Webb, Thomas Haggerty, the late Christine Marshall and Clyde Carter.

I want to thank my husband, Richard for always being there for me, pushing me to carry on when I want to give up, and for loving me and always taking care of me. I love you, honey. I want to thank my daughter, Chloe for being an awesome young lady. You are the reason why I work as hard as I do, you encourage me daily, you're my inspiration and I love you. To my son, Nick, I'm proud of you and I love you.

Thanks to my brother, Ty and his family: Ebony, Tyra and Elijah. I love you, guys. I want to thank the McLaughlin clan for accepting, embracing, loving me and allowing me to be a part of your family. I also want to thank my two sister/cousins, Monica Webb Foster and Destini O'Neill for always being there and supporting me.

Truly it takes a village to raise children, so I have to thank my aunts and uncles who helped lead, guide and direct me through life's journey. Donnie, Gloria, Robert Earl, Mark, Lynn, Ricky, and Pebbles, I love you all. Thank you to all of my great aunts, uncles, cousins, the Beckham family and

3

Marshall family members, play cousins and all who are connected to me, there are way too many of y'all to name.

I also have to thank my prayer partner and friend, Michael Brewster, who has helped keep me spiritually grounded and has always believed in me–even when I didn't believe in myself. I shall never forget the day you told me, "If you can get your mind to catch up with your blessing, you'll be okay." I got it, Michael, my mind caught up with my blessing, HALLELUJAH!!!!

To my circle of close girlfriends, Cheryl Massey, LaNitra Dyson Hymes, Ivana Jackson, Kristi Moore, Marvena Woods, Wilbert Connor, Mitzy Young, Kristiana Spencer, and my ride or die cousin and friend, Lisa Hunter Fields, I love y'all. To all of my 90 friends, we are family, it's too many of y'all to name. Love you guys too.

Love to my play auntie, Ms. Doris Butler, thanks for always being there for me, I love you to pieces.

Respect to my pastor, Pastor E.C. Wilson and First Lady Tammi Wilson. To my pastor friends that pray for me and encourage me: Bishop Ray Campbell, Bishop Robert Nichols Jr, Pastor Michael Clerkley, First Lady Clara Clerkley, Rev. Charles Webb, Rev. Homer Webb Jr, Pastor Isaac Harris and Prophet Munday Smith, who told me this day was coming. I shall always pay honor and respect to the late Dr. Homer D. Webb Sr. Love to my church family at Griggs Chapel Missionary Baptist Church and to the Sisters In Christ Book Club members. My circle of GCMBC girlfriends, much love to you.

4

I want to show love to those authors whom I admire: ReShonda Tate Billingsley, Victoria Christopher Murray, Kimberla Lawson Roby, Kim Cash Tate, Tiffany L. Warren, Stacy Hawkins Adams, Karen Kingsbury, Rhonda McKnight, Eric Jerome Dickey, the late Frances Ray, and the late E. Lynn Harris.

Special *special* thanks to Michelle Stimpson, my writing partner, prayer partner, mentor, role model and friend. I couldn't have done this without you. I love your spirit. You encourage me daily; thanks for taking me under your wing and for taking this journey with me. You are truly a blessing to me.

Last, but certainly not least, to you the readers, I pray that The Blended Blessings series is a blessing to you. Thanks for the love and support.

-CaSandra McLaughlin

Acknowledgments from Michelle Stimpson

I'm tremendously thankful to God for the gift of writing. Even more grateful for the faith to actually do the writing. The more I work with aspiring authors and fellow writers, I'm in awe of the creativity within each of us!

Thanks to my co-author, CaSandra. When we met that day at McDonald's, I really didn't know what you had in mind—but He is such a wonderful orchestrator! Thanks for allowing me the opportunity to learn how to grow other authors. It is my pleasure indeed.

Thanks again to Karen McCollum Rodgers for your editorial input.

Special thanks to my son for a brief bit of Army advice. Thanks to my "Black Christian Reads" sisters for the advice about the individual titles and the series titles. You ladies give sisters in the Lord a wonderful name!

Thanks to my husband, who has lost count of my books but continues to support me. You *are* the benefit, babe!

-Michelle Stimpson

CaSandra's Dedication:

For Chloe

Dreams come true if you work your dream.

Quitting is never an option!

~

Michelle's Dedication:

For my dad, Michael Music Sr.

Blending families is never easy.

Thanks to you, I didn't know that.

Chapter 1

I closed my eyes and opened them again to make sure I wasn't dreaming. I wanted to be sure that this beautiful 2 story, 6 bedroom, 3 full bath, 2 half-bath house was really mine. Darren had told me that he was ready for us to get settled in a house, but never in a million years did I think it would be like this. I'd seen gated communities on TV and even joked with Darren about living next door to Tyler Perry or even owning a home similar to T.I. and Tiny's. I never expected Lancing Springs, Texas to have houses this beautiful.

"Angelia, do you like it?"

"Oh my God, Darren, are you kidding me? I love it, honey and I love you too." I ran into his arms and planted a big kiss on his lips. "I can't wait to decorate every room."

"Come on, baby let's get unpacked; we can worry about decorating later. Amber, Marcus, come on, let's get these boxes in the house."

I stood there watching Darren unload the U-Haul truck. I took out my cell phone and decided to take a few selfies with our new house in the background. I couldn't wait to for all of my family and friends to see that I was *finally* getting it right. After two failed marriages, I *finally* understood that the good guy really is the best choice.

The first time around, I was married to my daughter Amber's dad, Javar Norell. Javar and I were only together for three years. I honestly thought that we would be together forever, that is, until he started drinking. Javar was a very spontaneous guy. He loved to hang out, take road trips and loved spoiling me with gifts, but I never knew how he was able to afford those gifts. I was so far gone that if Javar told me to jump, I asked how high. My mind was just gone, but that's what happens when you're young and in love.

Javar worked for a pest control company for a living, but after being with him for about a year I heard rumors pertaining to him selling drugs. Turns out, those "road trips" we were taking were actually drug deals.

One night Javar and his brother, Leo were at a party and the police raided the place. Javar got into a shootout with officers. He severely injured one cop and was shot by another. He survived the gunshot wound, but he might as well have been dead to me, because he's serving a life sentence without a chance for parole.

Witnesses said that Javar was about to surrender when the police started shooting at him. I was devastated and wanted some answers from the police but wasn't successful in getting them. When I gave birth to Amber several months later, I filed for divorce and moved on with my life.

That was seventeen years ago. Amber's a college-bound senior. She's the quiet, nervous type and she's a loner and that's probably because she was the only child for such a long time. Needless to say she's never given me any trouble and she helps me out a lot with Demarcus.

After Javar came Marcus or should I say *Mr. America.*

Marcus is good looking, a Tyrese look alike and he knows it. I've never in my life met a man who stayed in the mirror more than me. Marcus was a great provider and he fulfilled all my needs—and the needs of every other woman he met too. The funny thing about Marcus is that I would catch him cheating and he would lie and sweet talk me into staying with him. The final straw for me was when I found out he had a baby on the way. There I was all in la la land in love with him and so was Trisha; we were pregnant at the same time. Our children were born two days apart. My son Demarcus is eight years old now.

I made up my mind that I was done with love. I had planned to raise my children and be by myself until I met Darren. I remember going to Wal-Mart on an ice cream run. I absolutely love pecan pralines and cream ice cream and was having a serious craving. I threw on some sweats, a t-shirt and my baseball cap and went to the store. I went straight to the ice cream aisle and was livid when I realized they were out of my favorite ice cream. I guess Darren noticed the disgusted look on my face and it prompted him to come see what was going on.

"Is there something I can help you with? You seem to be upset?"

"Well unless you work for Bluebell, ain't a thing you can do for me."

I was truly irritated by him.

"Well you might be in luck." Darren reached in his basket and gave me his ice cream, my favorite, pecan pralines and cream.

I stood there with a huge smile on my face and I thanked him. He asked me for my number. At first I was a little hesitant but then thought, *Sure...why not.* Darren called me that night and we talked for hours. We even slept on the phone. I was so taken by him, I loved how we were able to share so much in just one night.

He told me about his previous marriage and about his twin daughters, Tyler and Skylar. Darren explained to me that he played professional football for two years but had to quit following a terrible knee injury. His ex-wife, Marcy was all for their marriage until he got hurt. Marcy started straying away from him and things around the house became tense. Darren is a family man so he tried to stay for the sake of his girls, but eventually the stress of being unhappy became too much for him to bear.

"I'm not going to lie," he admitted, "I could have been a better husband. But we were both in it for the wrong reasons to begin with, I think. Just young and stupid."

Of course, I could relate.

Darren and Marcy divorced and she and the girls moved to Lancing Springs. Darren threw himself into working as a supervisor at UPS. It wasn't the dream job but it's what paid the bills while he earned a teaching certificate and coached league football on the side. Because he'd been made wise investments with his NFL earnings, he was still in good shape financially. So while he knew that teaching wasn't the highest-paying career, the ongoing dividends from short and long-term investments would always provide a comfortable lifestyle.

Darren and I started dating and fell in love real quick.

I wasn't used to having a good man, so I had to learn to adjust. Darren is truly one of a kind so when he asked me to be his wife, there was no doubt in my mind that he was the one. Darren loves the game of football. Football is his life, which is why we're here in Lancing Springs. One of Darren's coaching friends told him about an opening for the assistant coach position here at the high school. Darren interviewed for the job and here we are. Although Lancing Springs is different from my hometown, Dallas, Texas, I'm sure I'll adjust. I can always go home to visit; it's only an hour away.

"Baby, what are you doing?" Darren interrupted my thoughts.

"I'm just admiring the house, still can't believe it's ours."

"Well believe it." He pulled me close and hugged me tight. "Mrs. Holley, I love you."

"I love you too, Mr. Holley. Or should I say *Coach* Holley?"

"Coach Holley. Babe, you don't know how good it feels to be here. This is a dream come true. I'm finally getting my chance to be a coach."

"Honey, you deserve it. You're going to help take this team to the playoffs."

"Babe, thanks for believing in me and standing by my side. Let's do a little more unpacking and then we'll grab a bite to eat."

"Okay, sounds good; I'll

go upstairs and check on the kids." Darren kissed me again and to my surprise, swatted my behind.

Demarcus cried, "Ewwww!" from the top of the staircase. He ran out of sight.

"You shouldn't have been spying!" I teased my son, though I was quite glad that he could now witness healthy affection between a man and a woman. I hoped that someday he would love his wife as much as I believed Darren loved me.

I was enjoying our moment until the phone rang.

"Baby, I'll get the phone, you go check on the kids."

"Hello," I practically sang into the phone.

"Hey Angelia, sweetheart, how are you?"

"I'm fine, Mother Holley we're trying to get settled in."

Vivian Holley is my mother-in-law. She is trying to get used to the fact that I stole her baby boy's heart and she also has an issue with this being my third marriage. When Darren and I married I started out calling her mom, but she insisted that I call her Mother Holley.

"Okay dear, I was just checking in with you all. I'm so happy for y'all; God is doing some great things for you and Darren so hopefully you can find a church for your family to join."

I try my best to tune Mother Holley out; every time I talk to her she shoves the church down my throat. Mother goes to church every other day and is involved in every ministry they have, from the Usher board to the Sunshine committee. I grew up in church but that wasn't my thing.

"Angelia, I think it's a great start and exactly what you need so when Darren gets custody of the girls you'll all be one big happy saved family."

"Custody of the girls!" I yelled before I knew it. My head was about to explode.

"Yes dear, that's part of the reason why Darren accepted the job, so that he can get custody of Tyler and Skylar."

I felt my blood boiling.

"Angelia, surely you didn't think that you moved into a house that huge just for your kids," Mother Holley said with an evil chuckle.

I was starting to sweat and needed to get off the phone with her before I said something I couldn't take back.

"Angelia, are you still there, dear? Didn't Darren talk to you about his plans?"

I could just wring this woman's neck; she knew good and well that I was clueless about this. I took a few deep breaths and replied,

"Umm … yes, we discussed it, but the decision isn't final as of yet. Mother Holley, I've got to go. Thanks for checking on us."

I hung up the phone before she could respond. *How could Darren keep something this important from me? Those girls can't move in and tear up my house.* Don't get me wrong, I like Tyler and Skylar, but living with them simply will not work. Skylar and Tyler are cut from a different cloth. I wouldn't call them ghetto, but they are a little unruly—but that's not *their* fault. Children do what they see, so in their case the apple don't fall far from the tree. It seems like every time Darren gets a call from Marcy, it's always about the twins fighting or getting expelled from school.

I'm so glad that my baby girl, Amber is nothing like those two. Amber is a straight-A student and wants to become an attorney. After learning about her father's questionable incarceration, Amber decided she wanted to be an attorney. She watches every TV show pertaining to law, especially after the Michael Brown and Eric Garner cases. Amber loves to read and she's never had a boyfriend. I'm hoping the move here will help her come out of her shell and I don't need those girls ruining my plans.

"Babe, Demarcus has his clothes unpacked and Amber's moping around, not really sure what's going on with her. Babe, did you hear me?"

"Oh honey, I'm sorry. I heard you, I was just deep in thought."

"Who was that on the phone?"

"Oh that was your mother calling to check on us. Let me go check on Amber so that we can go."

I climbed the stairs still heated about my conversation with Mother Holley. I had to find a way to ask Darren about the twins but not today. I wanted to enjoy my family and my beautiful house. I knocked on Amber's door but there was no answer. I entered the room and she was laying on the bed with her headphones on.

"Amber ... baby girl, why haven't you unpacked your

clothes?"

"Mom, I don't know. I'll get around to it."

"What's wrong?"

"I was feeling a little hot earlier and nauseous."

"It's probably from the excitement of the move and maybe even a little anxiety. You probably just need to eat something; come on, let's go. Darren wants to take us out to eat. "Mom, can you just bring me something back? I really just want to stay here."

"Okay baby, are you sure? Maybe we should take you to the doctor."

"No Mom, I don't need a doctor; you're probably right, it's the excitement of the move. I'll be fine. I'll shower and take a nap and when you guys return I'll be all better."

"Well okay, Amber, if you say so; call me on my cell phone if you need to."

"Okay Mom, I will." I kissed her cheek and left the room. Something didn't seem right. Maybe she was just nervous about the move. *Yeah, I'm sure that's all it is; otherwise, she'd tell me if there was a problem. Wouldn't she?*

Chapter 2

I tossed and turned all night long. I couldn't sleep because I couldn't stop thinking about what Mother Holley said. I rolled over and watched Darren as he slept. I loved watching him sleep. I snuggled up to him, laying my head on his chest so that I could hear his heartbeat.

"Ummmmmm, good morning, baby."

"I'm sorry I woke you up."

"No, don't be sorry. I have to get up anyway; I've got to go to the school for a few hours."

"Go to school for what, honey?"

"Coach Minden wants all of the coaches and players to come together for a meet and greet."

"Oh … okay, well I'd better get up and get breakfast started."

I kissed him and headed to the bathroom to wash up. I wondered why he hadn't told me about the meeting. *If he didn't tell me about that … Maybe Mother Holley was right. I've got to find a way to ask Darren if what she said was true. Maybe I'm jumping to conclusions. Darren and I have a solid strong relationship and I refuse to let anyone or anything come between us.*

I went into my beautiful gourmet kitchen to prepare breakfast and my mood immediately changed. My kitchen was fully loaded with two ovens, a microwave, dishwasher, coffee maker, toaster, freezer and refrigerator with an ice maker,

18

center island and a huge kitchen table. Darren even installed a system for me to play music.

I whipped out my new Rachael Ray pots and pans and turned on Pandora. Anita Baker was singing Rapture. I sang along "Caught up in the rapture of love." I swayed with the beat. "Nothing else can compare..." *They just don't make music like this anymore.*

I whipped up a feast for my family: bacon, sausage, eggs, toast, rice and made a small fruit platter.

"Babe, you got it smelling good up in here." Darren hugged me from behind.

"Well, I wanted to do it up right since this is our first official breakfast in our new house."

"Come here, girl."

Darren held me close as we danced to Jodeci's "Forever My Lady." We kissed passionately. I closed my eyes and moved to the music. I was loving every minute of it.

"Baby, I love you so much," Darren whispered in my ear.

"I love you too and I'm glad that we trust each other and that we don't have any secrets, right?"

"Right. There's no need for secrets."

I held him tighter. Mother Holley had it wrong. Darren would never keep a secret from me, especially not about something this important. *Old busy-body need to mind her own business. I refuse to allow her to steal my joy or mess up my happy family.*

"Mama, can I have some cereal?" Demarcus asked, breaking up our moment.

"No sweetheart, I cooked breakfast."

"Awwwwwwwwww man, I want some Apple Jacks."

"Where is Amber?" I asked.

"She's still in bed."

"I'd better go check on her."

"Babe, you can call her on the intercom; let me show you how to work it," Darren suggested.

Darren got an intercom installed so that I wouldn't have to yell upstairs for the kids. That's my man ... always looking out for me.

"Amber, good morning are you up?" I buzzed into her room.

"Mom, I hear you but I don't see you."

"I'm in the kitchen; come down for breakfast."

"Okay, be down in a few."

I got out my tableware that I had recently ordered from Barneys. I bought a pretty black and white Sarah Cihat set. I saw Claire Huxtable from *The Cosby Show* use the same set. Claire is the reason why I told Darren I had to have a formal dining room. Cliff and Claire made dining look like so much fun. *I just can't wait to host my first dinner party.*

"Mom, you really outdid yourself. Everything looks great," Amber said.

"Thanks, pumpkin. Alright, y'all, let's dig in."

We all fixed our plates and I couldn't help but notice that Amber only had fruit on her plate. Amber's always been a finicky eater, so I didn't bother her.

"Mama, can we go bowling today?" Demarcus asked.

"I think that's a great idea, honey. What time will you be back from the meet and greet?"

"I shouldn't be at the school for too long so let's go around 5:00."

"Okay, sounds great. The kids and I will go to Wal-Mart and pick up some more household supplies, then we'll be ready to bowl when you come back."

I got up and started clearing the table when the doorbell rang.

"Babe, I'll get it," Darren said.

"I wonder who it is ... maybe it's one of the neighbors."

I continued to clear the table and rinse the dishes until I heard Marcy's voice.

"Marcy, what are you doing here?" Darren asked nervously.

"You said you were going to get the kids today so I figured I'd bring them to you."

"Ahem." I cleared my throat to let them know I was standing there. Marcy stood there as if she didn't hear me ... like she was America's Next Top Model. She had on some black skinny jeans, and a shirt with the words "This Ain't What You Want" on it—oh, how I agree with that statement—and some black stilettos.

"Tyler, Skylar, go into the kitchen with Demarcus and Amber while I talk to your mother."

"Hello ladies," I said, since it was obvious that they hadn't planned to speak to me.

"Hey, Ms. Angelia," they   said in unison with an attitude.

I waited for the girls to be out of sight and then asked, "Marcy, who gave you our address?"

"I called Mom and she gave it to me."

"Mom? Who is Mom?"

"Oh yeah that's right, I forgot *you* have to call her Mother Holley," Marcy proudly pointed out.

"Look, I don't give a flying—"

"Whoa, whoa … wait a minute, let's all calm down," Darren interjected.

"Marcy, I have to work today and if you had called you would know that," Darren explained.

"I need a break; I have something to do, and since Little Ms. Sunshine ain't got no job, I don't see what the problem is. I'm sure she can take a break from fluffing pillows and hanging curtains … better yet, since y'all have new money, I'm sure y'all can afford a butler to help around here too," Marcy yelped.

"I got your sunshine right here." I moved toward Marcy like a raging bull.

"Ladies, ladies, ladies. Can't we all just get along?" Darren begged.

"You better talk to her about disrespecting me at my house."

"*Your* house? Girl, please. This is Darren's house, you just live here."

"I live here because I'm his wife, something you wish you still were. You're just jealous."

"Alright, that's enough!" Darren warned us both.

"Marcy, you can leave the girls here for tonight, but next time call first. Understand?"

"Yeah, whatever," she said and strutted out the door.

I felt my blood pressure rising. *I've never in my adult life felt like fighting anyone until today.* Marcy had me in an uproar.

"Darren, I can't believe that woman had nerve enough to come into my house and disrespect me. And your mother is out of order for giving her our address."

"Babe, calm down. I understand you're upset and rightfully so. I'll call my mother this evening and we'll get to the bottom of this."

"Now what am I supposed to do?"

"Just take the girls with you to Wal-Mart and we'll all go bowling this evening."

"Take them with me? Darren those girls barely spoke to me when they got here. Now you're asking me to spend the day with them!" I yelled, on the verge of tears.

"Honey, everything will be ok. I promise you this won't ever happen again." Darren kissed my forehead and then moved to my mouth.

"Okay," I said, still feeling uneasy.

"Alright baby, I'm leaving now. Call me if you need to," Darren said and left.

I went upstairs and got in the shower. I cried the whole time I was in there. Why was this happening to me? What did I do to deserve this? All I want is for me and my family to be happy. It seems like every

23

CaSandra McLaughlin & Michelle Stimpson

time I think things are going good, something always happens. Mother Holley and Marcy got another thing coming if they think I'm going to let them mess up my happy home.

I finished my shower and got dressed. I was not going to let Tyler and Skylar intimidate me in my own home. They may be unruly at their house, but today they'll act like they have some sense.

"Mom, are you okay?" Amber asked, hugging me.

"Yes, baby I'm fine. Let's go." I grabbed my keys and put on my Versace shades and walked out my room confidently.

"Demarcus, Tyler and Skylar, let's go!" I announced.

"Alright, Angie ... I see you with the fake Versace shades," Tyler laughed as she descended the staircase.

"My shades aren't fake, and that's Ms. Angelia to you," I said sternly.

We walked into the garage to get in my black, fully loaded, 2015 Lincoln Navigator.

"Oooh, this mug *sweet*. I'm riding shotgun." Tyler ran to the passenger side and got in.

"Yep, it's on fleek," Skylar chimed in.

"What does *on fleek* mean?" Amber inquired.

"Wow, you really are lame. It means on point. What a nerd," Tyler said, sounding irritated.

"There will be no meddling or name calling. Do I make myself clear?" I yelled.

"Yes ma'am," Tyler said in a very annoying tone.

I pulled into Wal-Mart and hoped that things would go

24

okay. I was determined to not let these girls drive me up the wall.

"Mama, can I go to the book section? I really want to get a new comic book," Demarcus asked.

"Why don't all of you go pick out a book? I'll shop and meet you up front."

There was a small spark in Skylar's eyes, but Tyler sassed, "I don't want no book. School is over with."

"Tyler, there are all types of books: Puzzles, teenage novels, even magazines with the latest artists in them and they come with posters too," Amber said.

"Do they have books on August Alsina?" Skylar asked.

"Probably."

"Oh snap, for real?" Tyler came to life. "'Cause he's gonna be my baby daddy."

"You tripping. That's *my* baby daddy," Skylar shouted.

"Girls, quiet down. People are starting to stare at us and both of you are too young to be talking about having a baby daddy. Amber, go ahead and take them to the book section and meet me at the front in 30 minutes," I said, feeling embarrassed. *I don't know why I'm surprised, because I'm sure they got this mess from Marcy.*

"Okay Mom, we will," Amber agreed.

I was so glad to have some me time, even if it was for only a few minutes. There was no way I was going to be stuck in the house with these girls until Darren got home. I took my time walking up and down each aisle. I was beginning to relax. *Maybe I can handle these girls. Maybe they'll get to know me and not judge me based on what their mother says. I've only been around the girls a few times, so this is really new to all of us.* I also reminded myself that Darren had accepted me and my children as a package deal. I owed it to him to at least try to get along with his children. The job would have been easier, of course, if their mother had sense.

I strolled down the detergent aisle and then made my way to the front. To my surprise the girls were behaving. I spotted them and waved for them to come and join me in line. I noticed that Tyler and Skylar both had magazines, a pair of tights and a tank top, while Demarcus and Amber only had a book each. I was floored at first but calmed myself down quickly. I knew that these twins were trying me. I placed all of the items on the register belt and paid for them.

I needed to waste some more time before meeting with Darren so we went to Target, Ross and stopped by Albertsons to pick up some groceries.

When we got to the car I decided to call Darren to see how things were going.

"Hey honey, how are things going with you and the girls?"

"Oh they're going," I said, trying to sound convincing.

"Look, babe, I appreciate everything you're doing; I know they can be a handful. I'll be leaving here in the next twenty minutes. There's a thunderstorm coming through, and outdoor practice got cut short today, so the boys are going to work on strength training in the gym. I'll just meet you at the bowling alley, okay?"

"Okay honey, sounds good."

"Angelia, I love you."

"I love you too."

I hung up the phone with a new attitude. I was glad that Darren's meeting was ending soon. I turned the music up to drown out the chatter of Tyler and Skylar talking about August Alsina and Usher. I looked in the mirror and noticed that both Demarcus and Amber had their headphones on and were reading their books.

I parked in the driveway and told the kids to stay in the car while I ran the bags in the house. There was no need for them to get out. I dropped the bags off, put away the items needing refrigeration, set the alarm and hopped back in the car.

"Mom, is Dad going to meet us at the bowling alley?" Amber asked.

"*Dad?* Girl, who you calling Dad? Ain't yo' daddy locked up?" Tyler laughed.

Amber tried to hold back her tears but couldn't.

"You're a bully, Tyler and you're dumb and stupid," Demarcus defended his sister.

I pulled the Navigator over, trying my best to remember that this was a child.

"Tyler, what you said was very rude and uncalled for. Amber knows that Darren isn't her biological father, but he wants her to call him dad. You might not like the fact that your father is remarried, but you will not disrespect me nor my children."

"You getting on Tyler, but what about Demarcus?" Skylar pointed out. Her tone was soft but firm.

"Skylar, you didn't let me finish, and you're wrong for butting in while I'm talking."

I continued, "Demarcus, you're wrong for calling Tyler dumb and stupid, so apologize."

"I'm sorry that I called you dumb and stupid."

"Tyler, now you apologize to Amber."

"I'm sorry," Tyler said, smacking her lips.

"I don't care if you like one another, but you will respect each other. Tyler and Skylar whether you like it or not, we're all family. I will be telling your father what happened." Hearing the teeth sucking coming from the back, I looked into my rearview mirror in time to see Tyler give Skylar the duck lips and side eye. I made sure to send both girls my stern-mother gaze, but Skylar, totally unaware of the eye war going on between Tyler and me had her eyes trained on Amber's book.

I pulled back onto the highway and headed to the bowling alley. The kids stayed silent the whole time. I didn't see Darren's Nissan Altima in the parking lot but decided we'd go ahead and get a lane. I refused to spend any more time in the car with these kids.

I reserved a lane and paid for shoes for everyone. The kids started bowling while I went to order pizza. Darren still hadn't arrived. I retrieved my cell phone from my new Louis Vuitton purse. The phone rang several times, no answer. I called back and it went straight to voicemail.

I decided to go ahead and join in with the kids; they were actually communicating without the drama. And they were enjoying ourselves. Tyler and Skylar made fun of the way I held the bowling ball, but other than that everything was fine. I took a break and checked the time. We had been bowling for over two hours and Darren still hadn't made it. Rain was pouring down, and thunder rattled the building slightly. I called Darren again and still didn't get an answer. I was getting worried but didn't want to alarm the kids.

"Alright, come on, you guys ... let's go home."

"Do we have to, Mama? I need one more strike to win," Demarcus whined.

"Where's Daddy?" Skylar asked, sudden concern showing in her eyes.

"He got stuck at the school, so he's going to meet us at the house," I said, trying not to sound nervous.

My mind was wondering like crazy. What if he got in an accident, what if he got robbed? I needed to get these kids to the house and then go by the school to see if Darren was there. The kids and I hurried to the car; my thoughts made me speed up. What should have been a twenty-minute drive to my house turned into twelve minutes, despite the rain. I clicked the garage-door opener to let the garage up and Darren's car was in the garage.

I marched into the house and there was a boy sitting at my kitchen table eating wings like he was at home.

"Excuse me, who are you

29

and what are you doing in my house?" I asked with my hands on my hips. I couldn't believe what I was seeing.

"I'm K. J. McDaniels and I play football for the Lancing Springs Tigers. Coach Holley brought me home with him."

"I see you've met K.J." Darren entered the kitchen, looking worried.

"Yes, we've met and I was waiting for him to tell me why he's here."

"Hey, Daddy, who is that? He fine." Tyler giggled.

"Young lady, watch your mouth and go upstairs with the rest of the kids," Darren scolded.

"Angelia, K.J's grandmother had a stroke and we've been at the hospital all afternoon."

"K.J., I'm sorry to hear about your grandmother; where are your parents?" I asked.

"Both of my parents died in a car wreck," K.J. said sadly.

"Honey, K.J will be spending the night with us tonight. He's going to sleep down here in the guest room."

First the girls get dropped off unexpectedly and now this football player is moving in. *We're not Motel 6; we won't be leaving the light on. Surely this little boy had some family members he could call. There are other coaches on the team that he could have stayed with. Why couldn't he stay with them?*

"Angelia … baby, did you hear me?" Darren asked.

"Yeah I heard you, I'm going to go upstairs and check on the kids."

Once inside my bedroom I found my nightgown and decided to take a hot bath. I needed relaxation in order to clear my mind. I lit some candles, turned on Pandora and let the smooth sounds of David Sanborn take me away. I had no intentions of dealing with the kids tonight. I decided to let Darren deal with the children because clearly he didn't need me. Darren and I needed to have a long talk because I didn't sign up for any of this.

Chapter 3

"Angelia, I know you're not sleep. Baby, please talk to me," Darren pleaded.

"Oh, so now you wanna talk?" I said sarcastically.

"What is that supposed to mean?"

"It means that I'm your wife and you are keeping secrets from me; that's what it means," I screamed.

"Angelia, please keep your voice down; I don't want the kids to hear us—and what secrets are you talking about?"

"I know you're not sitting here in my face acting like you don't know what I'm talking about."

"Babe, I don't want to argue with you. I apologized about Marcy coming unexpectedly … what more do you want me to do?"

"I want you to tell the truth. I want you to explain why you didn't tell me that you moved us here so that you could get custody of the girls."

Darren's head dropped. I reached up and turned on the night light above the headboard. He looked as if he was in a panic.

"Your mother told me that those are your plans; I just want to know at what point were you going to tell me?"

"Angelia … baby, I did mention to Mom that I wanted Tyler and Skylar to live with us. I think it would be good for them to have a wholesome, stable environment to live in. I don't see what the big deal is ... I accepted your kids," Darren pointed out.

"You accepted my kids ... what's *that* supposed to mean, Darren?" I said with major attitude.

"It means I love you and accepted you and them as a package deal; that's what you do when you're married. You're being hypocritical."

"It's not that I don't accept them, I just have to get use to them, Darren. Those girls put me through a lot yesterday, but you wouldn't know that because you weren't here."

"Baby, I'm sorry. I was headed home, but K.J. needed me. That's part of coaching too; the team is like family. I took him to the hospital to check on his grandmother."

"Honey, you just met K.J., why couldn't one of the other coaches take him?"

"I took him because it felt like the right thing to do; upon meeting him we clicked immediately. I feel like I've known him for a while. Angelia, you know I love you and I won't make any major decisions without talking to you. I was wrong for telling Mom about my plans before speaking with you, but it doesn't change the fact that I do plan to get custody of the girls. Me getting custody of the girls won't happen overnight, so I'm hoping that you will get use to having them around."

"There will have to be some changes, Darren and I mean some serious changes: they will have to respect me, not just me but Amber and Demarcus too."

"I know it's going to be an adjustment for us all when the time comes, but I promise you, baby, it's going to be okay. Have I ever let you down?" Darren pulled me into his arms and held me. All I wanted, for once in my life, was to be happy with my husband and my family in my house. I would try, for Darren's sake, to adjust to Tyler and Skylar, but as soon as they got out of hand, I would demand that he send them back to their mother.

"Okay, I'll try Darren; that's all I can do is try."

"That's all I'm asking you to do, baby." Darren gave me a quick peck.

"Honey, how long is K.J. going to be here?"

"Angelia, I honestly don't know. He called his uncle in Lubbock last night to tell him about his grandmother having a stroke. I am hoping that he'll be here today or no later than tomorrow. I don't want K.J. home by himself, worrying himself sick. So I plan to take him home to get some clothes so that he can stay here until then."

"Darren, that's another decision that you made without me. I don't want some strange boy parading around the house."

"Honey, K.J. won't be parading around the house. It's just for one more night and I will keep an eye on him; he's a good kid."

"How do you know what type of kid he is? You just met him." I said, rolling my eyes.

"Angelia, do you trust me?"

"Yes, I trust you, but this has nothing to do with trust. This is about you making decisions that affect my life without consulting me."

"Okay, okay ... I get it. I screwed up big time, and I'm sorry. I don't want to fuss all day, and from now on I will talk to you."

"You promise?"

"Yes baby, I promise. Now we better go downstairs and see what the kids are up to; I'm sure they're probably going to want some breakfast."

"I'll be down in a few; you go ahead," I said and smiled weakly.

I felt like I was in the twilight zone. I should have known something was going on, because Darren was too eager to get to Lancing Springs. I knew he wanted to be a coach, but I'm sure he could have gotten an assistant coaching position in another city. *I will not be starring in The Desperate Housewives of Lancing Springs. First thing Monday morning I am going to find me a job.*

Darren told me that I should wait until summer is over but I am going to the temp service. Darren's two-a-day practices start tomorrow, so I've got to hurry up and find something and fast. Surely he won't want the kids to be here alone. It's okay for Amber and Demarcus to be here alone, but adding Tyler and Skylar would be a disaster. That's it ... I'll find a job and then he'll have no choice but to only let the girls come over on the weekend from time and time, and he'll be here to deal with them, not me. Of course I'll have to deal with them too but not by myself. Yeah Darren, you may have a plan but I have a plan of my own.

I went into the closet and grabbed my laptop. I needed to send my resume to a few companies before tomorrow morning. I went on several job sites: Manpower, Office Team, Select Staff, Express Personnel, you name it … I sent my resume there. I was excited because all of them had Customer Service positions available. I had worked at USA Energy as a lead rep; that is, until I got laid off. I was at that company for eight years. I didn't look for another job, because I got laid off the week before Darren got the call for us to move here. I got my severance pay, 401k, and of course I automatically got unemployment. I really wanted to wait until after the kids went back to school before I started working but under the circumstances I needed a job like yesterday.

I decided that I better get downstairs before Darren came looking for me. I trotted down the stairs with a sense of accomplishment. I knew it would only be a matter of time before I started to hear from the temp services. I would be working and Tyler and Skylar would be out of my hair.

"Baby, I was just about to come and get you. Is everything alright?" Darren asked.

"Everything is just fine." I smiled.

"Glad to hear that. I'm about to take K.J. home; his uncle just called. I'm taking Demarcus with me. Amber's watching TV. Marcy is on her way to pick up Tyler and Skylar." Darren knew that was going to be my next question, so he beat me to the punch.

"Okay honey, what would you like for dinner tonight?" Excited that I would be getting the girls out of my hair soon, I planned to make him anything his heart desired. We would have the house to ourselves again and I could finally have some alone time with my hubby.

"Don't cook. I'll pick up some barbecue with all the trimmings and we'll just unwind and watch movies."

"Okay, sounds good to me," I said.

I walked Darren, K.J. and Demarcus outside and noticed that my neighbor was outside planting something. I knew someone lived next door but didn't know who. I decided I would go over and introduce myself.

"Hello. I'm your new neighbor, Angelia Holley, from next door."

"Hi baby, I'm Miss Earlene Jeffery. Good meeting you." She pulled me into a tight hug like we were close friends. Miss Earlene looked to be about 75 years old. She had on a duster, some tennis shoes with purple socks and a head rag.

"I just wanted to come over and introduce myself. What are you planting, if you don't mind me asking?"

"Chile, I'm planting some tomatoes and some cucumbers. I love planting … it eases my mind."

"How so?" I inquired.

"You see, being in the dirt reminds me of how we used to be until God saved us. We started as nothing but with God, we blossom into something. When we are watered with His word, we go through a lot of things, but He keeps on taking good care of us and we sprout up and

37

become what He wants us to be. I get joy from taking care of my tomatoes and cucumbers. They start out as a seed—oh hallelujah. I water them and they grow to be what I want them to be—glory to God. Ain't God good? He uses the smallest thangs to be a blessing to us."

"You got any chilren'?" she asked.

"Yes ma'am," I stuttered. "I have two children and two stepchildren."

"Chile, are you alright? What's on your mind?"

"Oh, nothing. It's just a little hot out here."

"Naw, you have *four* chilren'. You young folks don't know no better; when you get married, you become one, one in everything. If yo' husband got a car when you married, it's yours; if he got a house, it's yours and when he got chilren', they yours too. We 'spect men to 'cept our chilren' with no problem, but when it come to theirs, we get in a upro' and don't have a clue."

"Miss Earlene, I accept them, but they don't like me," I defended myself.

"Listen at you, chile; don't you know those chilren' just testing you? We test God patience every day with our ways. He chastise us and still love us—in spite of what we do—He keep on loving us. What if He looked at us as his stepchilren'?"

"Look I've got to go. Nice meeting you." I rushed back to my house.

Once inside the house I went into my den to sit and think about what Miss Earlene said. How dare this woman tell me about my situation with Tyler and Skylar? *She's probably the busybody of the neighborhood. Yeah, that's it,* I thought, trying to convince myself. I picked up the remote to thumb through the channels to find a movie to watch, but for some reason I just couldn't get Miss Earlene and what she said off of my mind.

Chapter 4

My heart raced with anticipation as I clicked on the email titled *Medical City Customer Service Rep.* Somehow, I found myself whispering, "Please, God," as my eyes scanned past the formalities of the email, which referenced the job code and my applicant ID.

Thank you for applying for the position through Springy Temps. Unfortunately... That was all I needed to see. "Shoot!" Well, it wasn't the first time my prayer hadn't been answered.

"This is ridiculous!" I fussed to myself as I logged into LinkedIn. There could not be that many qualified professionals in Lancing Springs, TX to knock me out of the running for a simple receptionist's job. *Really?* I was overqualified for most of Springy Temps' postings anyway. "They don't know me." I carried the laptop from my bedside to the antique oak desk in the office space just past our bathroom. It was time to get down to business. It'd been two weeks since I started my search and I seriously needed a job. It was time to broaden my search. That might mean a commute, but anything was better than feeling like a stay-at-home wife, mom, and stepmom.

A rap on my door interrupted my self-promoting party. "What?" I yelled at whoever was on the other side.

Amber poked her head through my bedroom door. "Mom."

I cocked my head to the side. "Yes?"

Her hair was pulled back into a studious-looking ponytail. "Um...I...I can see you're busy."

I nodded. "Yes. I am."

Her eyes dropped to the floor. "Okay. I'll come back later."

"Yeah. In another hour or so. Your momma is busy getting her life together."

I focused on the computer screen again, certain that Amber would close the door behind her. One thing I appreciated about Amber most was her self-sufficiency. She'd been the only child of a single mother for several years, which brought its own life lessons. I couldn't be there for her every moment of the day. Unlike Demarcus, Amber learned to take care of herself early in life. Amber's ability to handle business would soon pay off in scholarships that would earn her the degree I never got so that, hopefully, she would never end up in my shoes, scraping for the types of entry-level positions available to every Tom-Dick-and-Harry without a degree.

After another half hour of searching for openings, tweaking, copying, pasting, and sending out resumes for various posts, I was intellectually pooped. Yet, I googled to find a few more job-search tips since I'd been out of the job-hunting game for a while.

My research prompted me to upload a five-year-old throwback picture to my profile. When employers said they wanted "energetic" candidates that was the code word for "young." I also recognized that "dedicated" meant "married to the job," but I wasn't willing to hide all my photos of our wedding, at least not until we finished paying off all the credit cards.

Just as I was preparing to

shut down my computer and catch up with Amber, my inbox dinged with a message from someone named VARRIS regarding a data entry position in the next town over.

I clicked the message. Turns out, VARRIS stands for "Virtual Automated Resume Reader Innovation System." Apparently, some new technology had already assessed my resume and determined from the headings on my resume that my background and experience were not a good match for the posted position.

What? How on earth did a *machine* read my resume and decide not to hire me? "Ain't this a—"

"Momma!" My son's scream saved Ms. Varris from a good cussing-out.

I hopped up from my seat and rushed toward my door. "Demarcus, why are you hollering like you've lost your mind?"

"Doorbell!"

I wrapped my robe around my waist, pushing past him on the winding staircase. "Next time, use the intercom."

"I don't know how."

"Learn it!" I snapped back.

Through the beveled glass of our front door, I could see three figures. Three female figures. It only took a second for me to recognize them as Marcy, Tyler and Skylar.

I yelled through the door. "Yes?"

"It's me. With the girls," Marcy said.

"Darren's not here. You should have called first anyway," I

yelled clearly through the crack.

"Open the door. It's an emergency."

Fear shot through me. The last time someone said those words to me, my life had taken an unmistakable left. I quickly twisted the locks to the right and swung the door open expecting to see traces of tears rolling down Marcy's cheeks.

But Marcy's cheeks were perfectly brushed with rosy blush. Eyeliner intact. Weave flowing without interruption. I checked this women out from head to toe: skin-tight black dress with slits on the sides showing her hips and waist, a gold ankle bracelet and red bottom shoes. As much as I couldn't stand this woman, I had to admit to myself that she was still strikingly beautiful.

I tucked a loose wisp of hair under my scarf. "What's the emergency?"

"I have to go somewhere."

"Where?"

Marcy smacked her lips. "I'm a full-grown woman. I don't have to explain myself to you."

I tied my robe tighter and stepped outside on the porch. Marcy was about to catch what Varris barely missed. I gave the girls a quick glance. "Could you two go wait in the car? Your mother and I need to have a conversation."

They looked to Marcy. She told them to wait in the car.

We both watched them as they walked back to the driveway and hopped into Marcy's SUV. Beyond our hedges, I could see the top of Miss Earlene's gray wig. She must have been out working in the garden again.

Once Tyler and Skylar were safely out of earshot, I looked Marcy dead in her eye and said between gritted teeth, "Look. Darren is a very sweet, loving man. Those girls are his heart and he regrets every day that he hasn't been there for them, physically speaking. I, on the other hand, do not carry that same baggage."

Marcy crossed her arms and leaned to the side. "Well, I—"

"No, no. I'm not finished."

"I haven't even started!" she raised her voice.

I took a deep breath.

I heard a window on Marcy's car descend. Not willing to expose the girls to this drama, I tried again to lower the volume of our conversation. "All I'm saying is, I'd like for us all to be respectful and civil toward one another. Let's not make this harder than it has to be. You can start by not coming over here without calling first."

She rolled her eyes. "How do you know I haven't already spoken to Darren?"

"Excuse me?"

"We *do* talk, you know. These are *our* girls. And I've spent the past ten years raising them by myself while he went off doing his own thing in Dallas. Now it's time for me to have a break."

"A break? You don't get a break from being a parent," I fussed. "Not until they leave for college."

"Whatever. All I know is, Darren moved here to help me with the girls."

"He got a new job."

"There are hundreds of coaching jobs in Texas. Why do you think he applied for one in lil' ole' Lancing Springs? Ain't nothin' out here. Well, at least nothing on my side of town." She looked up and over my shoulder, visually surveying. "But obviously they're building up on *this* side. They opened a new *magnet* high school and everything. Your daughter—what's her name, Amira? Ambrosia?—enrolled yet?"

"It's *Amber*, and she's already been *accepted* Thank you very much. This school is not open to everyone in this zip code."

"Whatever. Just like you want the best for *your* kids, I want the best for mine. And so does Darren."

Marcy's words brought a fresh wave of anger over me. Now, for the second time, someone was telling me about my husband's plans to expand our newly formed family.

She must have read the shock on my face. She clapped her hands and bent over laughing like somebody high on crack, tongue sticking all out. "Whooo! Mrs. Angelia Holley, looks like the joke is on you."

"No. They're not staying here tonight. Not until Darren comes back."

Marcy blinked. "Yes. They are."

"No. They're not." I reached behind me and closed the door.

"We can call Darren right now." Marcy pulled her phone from her bra.

What if she's telling the

45

truth? Given what I already obviously didn't know about my husband, I didn't want to risk him making me look like a fool again on my own front porch.

"Never mind. We can settle this later. What time will you be back to pick them up today?"

"It'll be tomorrow."

"Oh, no it won't. We have plans tomorrow," I lied.

"Well, I have plans tonight and if all goes as planned, they won't be finished until the morning."

"What kind of an example are you setting as a woman for the girls?"

"Don't judge me." Marcy gave me the hand. "I'm working on husband number two. Trying to catch up with you. Whatchu on—number three, right?"

"Leave. Now." When I tell you I could have snatched her right there, I am not lying. But it's kind of hard to snatch somebody when you're really not sure what's the truth or who exactly to be mad at.

She motioned for the girls to get out of the car. They had barely closed their doors when she threw the car in reverse. "Text your Daddy. Tell him you're here."

"Okay, Momma. Bye." They waved as Marcy drove away in her Escalade which sounded more like an old Subaru.

She needs to hurry up and find number two with that old raggedy Cadillac.

The girls approached me in silence. Once they reached the porch, they simply stood as though I was supposed to open the door, like a servant.

"A hello would be nice," I said.

Skylar flicked her braids around and asked her sister, "It's our house, too, right?"

Before Tyler could agree, I answered, "No. A house belongs to the people whose names are on the mortgage. That would me and your father. Not you two, not Amber, not Demarcus. Only the people who pay the bills. And if you want to come inside someone else's house, it's common courtesy to at least speak to the owner first. So let's try this again. Hello."

"Hello," they muttered.

I opened the door. They entered and went upstairs to the rooms that had, apparently, been planned for them all along.

I rested the back of my head on the wooden doorframe.

It was time for me and Darren to have a talk.

Chapter 5

While getting dressed, I texted Darren twice about the twins' unexpected visit. When he didn't reply, I figured Marcy must have been right. Skylar and Tyler coming over wasn't a surprise to him. *I guess I'm the only one who didn't get the memo.*

Within fifteen minutes of my stepdaughters entering the house, I already heard "Shut up!" and "Get out!" shouted from both girls to Demarcus. Granted, my child could be annoying. He was a boy. He was eight. But there was no need for all this hollering.

I stormed over to the intercom, pressed the "ALL" button and yelled into the system, "Don't make me come in there!" Never mind the fact I wasn't quite sure where 'there' was in our spacious home.

These kids are getting on my last nerve and it's not even ten in the morning yet.

Of course, if I'd had a job, this wouldn't be a problem. Customer service could be a 24-7 job, depending on where I got hired. Since my first few attempts at finding work hadn't panned out, I'd resorted to broadening the proximity, lowering the salary requirements, and widening the breadth of what I might consider. Anything was better than this.

And Darren. More than anything, I wanted to have a good old-fashioned pow-wow with him. But the truth was: I was afraid. This wasn't my first rodeo. My marriage to Amber's father ended with him going to prison. But even if he hadn't been incarcerated, our relationship was on its way down the tubes. We fought constantly in those final months.

My second marriage was marred with secrets, half-truths, lies, arguments, cussing, me throwing stuff, him punching holes in the wall. Just crazy!

I didn't want this debate about Darren's girls to be the beginning of the end for me and my third husband. He and I had only been together six months before we married. We'd only been married a year when we moved into the house. Everything had been going better-than-fine before we moved here.

I didn't want to think my third husband was the kind of man who'd move me to a big 'ole house in a lil' country town so I could raise his girls. If I'd fallen for Mr. Wrong *again* dressed up in a different disguise, what kind of fool did that make me? Seriously, if it didn't work out between Darren and me, I'd just check myself into a hospital, because I'd be absolutely certain there was something wrong with me.

I brushed my cheeks with blush, thinking, *Am I that stupid?*

"I'm gonna tell my mom!" Demarcus's voice rang through the house, followed by the clunk-clunk of his feet taking the steps two at a time. "Momma!"

I called it quits on the makeup and met him at the top of the staircase. "What is it, Demarcus?"

"Skylar and Tyler are watching a Rated R movie."

"No we're not!" They denied in unison from the game room.

"Turn off the TV. We're going shopping in ten minutes. Everybody."

I'd commissioned Darren to put a parental block on the remote control to the television, but he'd been so busy with two-a-days he hadn't bothered yet. And now *my* children were in danger of being exposed to Lord-only-knows-what, thanks to those fast twins who, by this point in their lives, had probably sent some little boys a few R-rated texts. Given their mother's way with men, I wouldn't put anything past them.

I rushed to the kitchen and grabbed two granola bars. One for myself, the other for Demarcus's bottomless pit. Not the breakfast of champions, I knew, but I was in no mood to cook.

My phone dinged with a text. Elated at the possibility that Darren was finally contacting me, I quickly pulled it from my pocket.

But the first line showed it was from Amber. *Do I have to go?*

Normally, I thought less of people who texted each other while in the same house. But in that moment, a sense of pride swept over me as I realized the fact that we lived in a house big enough to actually justify texting from one room to another.

Picking out furniture for the guest rooms I need your decorator's eye ☺.

She sent: Don't feel like being bothered with everyone.

To which I initially typed. *Me either*, but I cleared the message. This was my drama, not Amber's. *OK. But if I pick out some foolishness, it will be your fault.*

You'll be fine, Mom. Talk to you later?

K.

I'd forgotten about my promise to carve out some time for her, so I made myself a mental note to touch bases with her when I got back home, or at least as soon as I got rid of Skylar and Tyler. They needed constant supervision. What they really needed was their Daddy, but there was no telling what time he'd come back from an all-day coaches' conference where, according to him, they'd be discussing player safety and new NCAA rules.

He'd tried to explain the significance of his coaching team sending him as a representative. "Baby, I'm working in Lancing Springs now. We've got a promising program, a strong feeder pattern, and some really good athletes whose parents can afford to send them to camps and put them on elite teams. It's different. Scouts are looking at the boys, but they're also looking at consistent programs. I might even coach at the college level one day."

"Whoop-tee-doo," I said as I pulled the covers over my ears.

That was the last thing I said to him last night. He had kissed me. Tried to make me talk. But again, I feared if I unleashed the raging torrent inside, our relationship might get swept away in the current.

I'd said enough already. The silent treatment did the rest of my talking for me, which was probably why Darren had left without even saying good-bye.

This is a mess.

Darren was gone and now I was taking Demarcus and the twins shopping without the aid of Amber. *This is about to be mess number two.*

With Demarcus in the front seat, away from the twins, the ride to The Last Look Furniture Warehouse was quite uneventful. But when I pulled into the parking lot, Skylar fussed, "This ain't *shopping*. This is a *furniture* store."

"People do shop for furniture."

"Do we have to get out?" Tyler asked.

"Yes, ma'am. Everybody's getting out."

"But you're not shopping for us."

"I'm not leaving you in a hot car, either," Angelia reasoned.

"Just leave the keys in," Tyler suggested.

"Over my dead body." Angelia parked and unlocked the doors. "Out."

The girls' tunes changed once they entered the superstore. Almost immediately, they ran to the staged master bedroom and hopped onto an ornately decorated king-sized bed. They spread out like they were making snow angels.

"Oh my gosh! This bed is so awesome!"

Demarcus tried to join them, but I quickly grabbed his hand. I rushed to the model and said as loudly as I could without sounding too out-of-control, "Get off of that bed."

The girls leaned up, halfway ignoring me, and looked around the warehouse. "Oh! This place is amazing!" Tyler exclaimed. "Which rooms are you shopping for?"

"The guest rooms. Now, get up."

"Wait. Our rooms?" Skylar squealed.

I clarified, "The rooms you'll stay in when you *visit*."

"Eeeek! Yes! Oh my gosh, Skylar, let's find the perfect bed!"

"Don't get carried away," I suggested.

"I'm gonna text Daddy a picture of this bed. I love it." Tyler snapped a shot before I could kindly inform her that her father was too busy to pay attention to texts from family this morning.

"Ooh! Look at that one over there; that's the one I want for my room!" Skylar pointed to a pink and white bunk bed set.

"Momma, I want a bunk bed," Demarcus cried.

"You don't need a bunk bed. You don't have a twin," Tyler squashed his hopes. "You don't even have friends. Why would you need a bunk bed?"

"I do have friends. The only reason you got a friend is 'cause you got a twin. She didn't have a choice!" he smarted off.

Ooh, I wanted to give him a high-five, but I didn't want to be too ugly.

Tyler's phone chimed. She looked at the screen, then said to her sister, "Dad says it's too big for the room. Find something smaller."

Oh, he's replying to texts now? "Tyler, tell your father to call me, please."

She sent the message.

"If you two promise to behave, I'll let you look around the store for yourselves." The store had an open concept, which would allow me to keep an eye on them while I gave their father a piece of my mind.

They scrambled off to the right. I let Demarcus wander to the left while I waited for Darren's call.

Chapter 6

I waited in a wing-backed La-Z-Boy, hoping the sides would keep the general public from overhearing the tongue-lashing I had prepared for my husband. I rehearsed the speech in my mind: *How you gonna return your daughter's texts but not mine? Why am I here with them again anyway? If you think for one minute I'm going to take over your parental responsibilities while you chase your coaching dreams all over Texas, you got me messed up!*

Instead of a call from Darren, Skylar sent me a message. *Said he tried 2 call you but yo phone went 2 voice mail.*

I checked my signal. None. Those little country towns played favorites with the cell phone carriers.

Saved by the bars.

A young Hispanic couple walked by, hand-in-hand, browsing the chairs. I sat back and watched as the husband and wife walk the aisles, taking turns testing seat cushions. They smiled at each other. Bounced on the chairs, laughing and sharing private jokes. Between each test, they held hands again, unwilling to be separated for long.

That's how you're supposed to shop for furniture. With your spouse!

Granted, I had shopped for furniture alone before—when I was single. But if I was going to have to live like a single mother—this time with *four* kids—Darren could take that big old house and...wait. No. He couldn't have my house. We're going to have to work something out.

I started thinking about child support, but since he never adopted Demarcus or Amber, that wasn't going to happen. *I'd need three jobs to keep the house. Maybe I'll go back to school. Shoot, I won't be finished before they foreclose.*

Wait! Why am I thinking like this! I sank deeper into the chair, wondering what was wrong with me. All the research I'd read on second and third marriages had said that the occurrence of divorce was higher after the first marriage because people are well-versed in throwing in the towel. But Darren and I had decided that *we* would be different. *We* would make it, despite the odds. I believed in him. I believed in us. I just didn't believe there would be an "us" if he was never around. *Maybe this was the real reason why he and Marcy divorced.*

I hid my eyes behind my hand and tried to persuade the tears to stay put, but they wouldn't listen. I wiped them away as quickly as they came, hoping none of the sales people would approach me again. I wasn't in the mood to make any major purchases under these circumstances. For all I knew, I might have to sell this stuff to pay rent somewhere in another six months.

"Boo!"

I jumped at my son's successful attempt to surprise me. "Boy, quit playing!"

Satisfied that he'd scared me out of my skin, he threw his head back in laughter, which gave me enough time to compose myself. "I got you!"

56

"Yes, you did." I threw my purse handles over my shoulder and stood. "Where are the girls?"

"I don't know. Momma, I gotta show you this bed."

I allowed Demarcus to drag me to the children's section, though his bedroom was nowhere on the shopping list. We stopped at a wooden full sized bed with a Dallas Cowboys logo on the circular headboard. My son posed like Hercules. "All for me!"

I laughed, slightly amused by his antics. Demarcus took the liberty of showing me around the fake room. "Look under here!"

He pulled out the three trundle drawers below the Cowboy's bedspread. Next, he showcased the nightstand, football lamp, and a dresser and mirror/corkboard combination. "The wood is amazingly shiny," he said, stroking the footboard. "So beautiful, this room makes the person who owns it want to keep it clean."

I had to do more than grin on that one. "Demarcus, you are silly!"

Once he saw his magic working on me, he asked, "So, Momma, you think I can get this room?"

"There's nothing wrong with the room you have now," I said.

"But...I don't know. I was thinking ..." His smile slipped, gave way to a more serious expression. "Maybe if I have, you know, a *football* room, one of my Dads would spend more time with me."

My heart screeched to a

halt as I watched my baby try to cover his true emotions with a half-smile.

I swallowed. Pulled his head to my side so he wouldn't see my face. Cleared my throat. "Don't worry, baby. Things will get better as soon as football season is over."

We left the furniture store and picked up lunch, but those words from my son wouldn't leave me. I know from my own experience that children internalize their parents' neglect. This issue with Darren was bigger than me, now.

I watched passively as Demarcus and the twins semi-argued throughout their meals. He really didn't hate them. They really didn't hate him, either. They were just eight- and thirteen-year-old kids, and that came with its own baggage. Of course, Skylar and Tyler had a little more. But if I stayed with Darren, Demarcus might have more issues, too.

My mind raced through a worst-case scenario. If I left Darren, Demarcus would become bitter, an angry black boy. Then he'd start being disrespectful to his teachers, getting into fights at school, talking back to me. Then I'd have to knock the black off of him. Then somebody would call Child Protective Services about his missing teeth. Demarcus would have to go live with his father, but Amber could stay because she'd be 18 by then. My ex-husband would be too busy running the streets and chasing women to watch our son, so my baby would start hanging with the wrong crowd. Doing drugs. He'd join a gang. Start robbing people on the streets. Get shot in a bank hold-up, and then—

"Miss Angelia!" Tyler yelled my name as though I wasn't sitting across from her in a booth at Chick-fil-A.

"Hu ...what?" I snapped back to reality, blinking away tears.

"My Daddy said he's about to call you on your phone."

"Oh. Okay."

My phone vibrated. I answered, "Yeah?"

"Hey. I'm on lunch break. What's up, baby?"

"What's up?" I repeated, stepping out of our booth. I mouthed to the children *I'll-be-right-back*, then slipped into an empty booth on the other side of the condiment stand. "What's *up* is how Marcy dropped off the girls without anyone giving me any kind of notice. Demarcus trying to get a football bedroom set so he can be closer to you, and me wondering if this marriage is going to work out!" I cried.

"Slow your roll, baby. Rewind. What's wrong?"

The concern in his voice rang true. I knew Darren wasn't really going to be a neglectful husband and father, but he sure was acting like one. "I thought we were moving to Lancing Springs to start our new family *together*. I knew we'd see the girls more often, but Marcy's taking advantage of how close we live to her now. And your new job is more like your new wife than I am."

"Calm down, boo." The deep timbre of his voice brought comfort to my shivering insides. "I'm so sorry, babe. I'll have a talk with Marcy. Okay?"

I sniffed. "Okay."

"And you know the only

reason I'm working so hard is to provide for our family, right? Isn't that what a man's supposed to do?"

He had a point. "Yes, but—"

"Then let me do my job," he insisted. "I'm trying to make a good first impression this year."

"Does it take a whole year to make a good first impression?"

"In sports it does," he said.

I blew air out of my mouth. "I don't know how much—"

"Don't even say that." He stopped me. "I gotta go. Talk to you when I get home?"

"What time will that be, Darren?"

"I'm not sure. I'll let you know when we leave the workshop. You gonna wait up for Big Daddy?"

His flirting might have made my stomach tingle, but I couldn't let him off that easily. "Big Daddy better get home before I shuts it down."

He laughed. "Love you."

"Love you, too."

Our two-minute conversation settled my imagination long enough to take on the home and garden store. Now that Skylar and Tyler had been with me for a while, they seemed more tolerable, helping me pick out bath rugs and towels to fill the empty linen closet in the guest suite. I figured that after my meltdown, Darren might have texted them and told them to behave.

Upon our return home, the kids hopped out and went inside

while I moseyed on down to meet our postal carrier. She was chatting with Miss Earlene at the mailbox station between our homes. The mail carrier was an elderly African-American woman who seemed too old to still be working—especially outside on a hot, Texas summer day.

"Jackie, this here is Angelia," Miss Earlene introduced us over the hum of the mail truck's engine.

"Nice to meet you," I said, reaching through the open side to shake Jackie's hand.

"Same here. Nice house you got here. I've been running mail in Lancing Springs almost thirty years. Glad to finally see *us* on this side of town." Jackie rubbed the back of her brown-skinned hand at the word *us*.

I smiled at her.

"How many kids you got?"

"I have two. The other two are my husband's."

"Oh. Twins, huh?"

"Yes, ma'am."

She looked back toward my doorway, as though recalling Skylar's and Tyler's facial features. "They from Lancing Springs, right?"

"Yes, ma'am," I confirmed.

"Hmmm. They wouldn't happen to be kin to the Covingtons, would they?"

"Actually, yes," I said. "Their mother is Marcy Covington."

"Chile," Jackie said under her breath. She got busy stuffing the three open mailboxes with junk mail. "I know you got your hands full with them two 'cause Marcy's momma had her hands full with Marcy. Me and Marcy's Momma, Genine Covington, we graduated high school together. All their family problems go *way* back."

I had fixed my lips to ask for more information when Miss Earlene interrupted, "Watch out now, Jackie. You know I don't do gossip."

I do.

Jackie chuckled. "Earlene, you always have been a *real* church woman. Can't talk bad about anybody around you."

"You got that right." She nodded in a way that maintained her good humor but still shut down Jackie's flow of information. "People do better when they know better. Until then, don't do no good to talk about 'em like dogs."

Jackie rolled her eyes. She wiped her forehead. "Let me get back on my route. Good seeing you, Earlene, and meeting you, Angelia."

"Same here."

The sun bore down on Miss Earlene and me heavily. I slid the mail out of our receptacle. "This heat is for real," I said.

"Sure is," Miss Earlene agreed as she thumbed through envelopes. "Listen here, don't you pay too much mind to what Jackie said."

"Well, she *does* have a point." I fanned myself with a 5x7 postcard.

"But my point is: Kids ain't got no control over what their parents do. Even if those girls' momma is wild, don't mean they have to turn out that way. You get 'em in church, they got a chance."

I would gladly give those heathens to anybody's church if I knew of one. "I'll see what I can do."

"We got Vacation Bible School coming up at our church next week. Part of our back-to-school rally. Bus comes right by here to pick me up, since I teach the pre-teens. They'll take all yours, too. Good people at my church, no funny business. I can call Brother Presley and make sure they got enough room, but—"

"Oh, no. Thanks for the offer, Miss Earlene, but we're fine."

She tilted her head down. "Look. I raised six kids. Four of my own, plus my sister's two. I know a worn-out Momma when I see one. Send 'em to church while you go get your nails done. Get your hair done." She eyed my baseball cap. "Take a little time for yourself."

Music to my ears. "What time does the bus come?"

I tried to wait up for Darren, I really did. But when he texted me at eleven saying they still had another hour's drive, I already knew I wasn't going to get lucky that night.

I refreshed my Facebook page one more time to get the latest trends. Nothing interesting. I typed: *Nite FB family.*

And then the number one appeared by my Friend icon. I clicked the silhouette and waited a second for the requestor's name to appear.

Sherman Johnson.

Oh my gosh! Sherman Johnson! I quickly accepted his request and checked his "About" page. Besides what I already knew—the year of his birth, where and when he finished high school, and his college degree—everything was blank. *Is he still married to that skank, Tameka Dunsey? She was never good enough for him.* There were pictures of him and a little boy, him and what must have been co-workers. I scrolled back to the previous year and saw pictures of him and a Tameka who still looked like a circus clown with all that makeup, but none recent. How he picked her masked-face over me, I'll never understand.

Let the record show: *He* requested *my* friendship that night. *Old Sherman Johnson.*

Chapter 7

Upon the "advice" of Darren's boss, Coach Minden, my husband informed me that we were to host a Labor Day back-to-school barbecue.

"What?!" I fussed.

"It's kind of like an initiation. The new coach does it his first year," he said as he followed me around the kitchen like a stray dog hoping for a morsel of food.

I stopped chopping the onions and set the knife on the cutting board just in case my hands forgot to stay calm. "You and I are like two ships passing in the night since we moved into this house. I barely see you. And now you want me to throw a happy-go-lucky party for you and all the rest of the coaches' families?"

He stepped into my personal space and slipped his arms around my waist. "Baby. You said you wanted more family time, right?"

"Yes. Family time with me, you, and the kids," I said, poking his shoulder three times to emphasize my point. "Not the whole darn neighborhood." Three more pokes.

"I know. But really, babe, the coaches and their families will be like our extended family during football season. You *are* coming to the games, right?"

"Yes," I assured him, though I wasn't exactly excited about the idea of sitting in the heat during those earlier games or shivering under a blanket during the winter games if they made it to the playoffs. Texas weather was one of the main reasons I only signed Demarcus up for indoor soccer or basketball.

"Well, when you come to the games, Coach Minden's wife will have seats saved for you and all the coaches' families. That's one of her duties."

"Duties? What's *my* duty?"

"Come to the games and cheer us on. Give me a thumb's up when we're down." He kissed my forehead. "That's what I need."

I promise, if his skin wasn't such a deep, savory chocolate and his lips weren't quite as soft and decadent, there's no way I would have sent out those Evites to his teammates and made those arrangements with the caterers. Nonetheless, Darren was quite the charmer. And there I was two weeks later hosting a team barbecue-slash-housewarming party. I figured since we were opening up to visitors, we might as well invite family and friends.

My family would probably be on its best behavior so long as there were white people present, so this was the perfect time to invite my cousins Erica and Claudia. Their mother, my Aunt Viola, took me in and finished raising me when my mother passed away of cancer. I was seventeen and a junior in high school. Erica and Claudia were also juniors. They weren't twins, though. They were eleven months apart. One born in September, the other in July, which put us all in the same grade at Robertson High School. I tried my best not to let anyone know they were related to me because they were so loud, rude, and always in some he-said-she-said mess.

Still, they were family. Despite their Real-Housewives ways, they've always had my back—even if just to keep a nose in my business.

I knew Uncle Earl and Aunt Mazie weren't coming. They don't travel ten miles outside of Marshall unless there's a slot machine awaiting. Country folk and their country ways.

Erica and Claudia didn't RSVP, but I knew they wouldn't miss the opportunity to come and see what kind of house my new man had bought me. They simply showed up around 8:30 p.m. with two men in tow.

"Ooooh, girl!" Claudia exclaimed as she pushed past me and into the foyer. "He make *this* kind of money coaching high school football?" She slapped her man in the stomach with her patent leather clutch bag. "Boo, you in the wrong business."

"Hello," I said, raising arms to hug my cousins.

"Hey, honey," Claudia squealed. She shuffled her high heels over to hug me. I swear she acted just like Niecy Nash.

"Lookin' good," Erica said, joining our group hug. "Y'all didn't waste no time getting out of Dallas, huh?"

"None at all," I said. Her generous helping of perfume rushed up my nostrils. Good thing it wasn't cheap.

Then again, Claudia and Erica always had expensive tastes. They lived the rich-on-Friday-poor-by-Wednesday lifestyle; where you drive a BMW but can't afford to fix its cracked windshield. They both had good jobs and could manage a low-key lifestyle if need be, but they preferred a man's company and financial contributions to   put them over the break-even line.

I couldn't judge, though, because really, what woman *couldn't* use the cushion of an extra check in the household?

They introduced their boyfriends as Chris and Rolando. Both men had clean-shaven heads and wore crisp woven shirts with shorts. Nice-looking. Wouldn't expect anything less from my cousins.

After a grand tour of the house, filled with their "oohs" and "aaahs" and Claudia outright collapsing on my bed in straight drama-queen mode, we joined the rest of the guests outside on the covered patio.

The sun had relented from its torturous job and left us with a decent evening temperature. Darren lit the mosquito lamps stationed around our quarter-acre back yard. Our guests, full from the food we'd all devoured half an hour earlier, were lounging in chairs, talking among ourselves, laughing loudly while taking pictures.

I introduced Darren's colleagues and their wives to my cousins. Amber and Demarcus gave Claudia and Erica hugs, which made my heart smile a little. I wanted my kids to know their blood-relatives because if anything ever happened to me, they'd probably end up with one of these two ladies.

Darren greeted my cousins and their dates warmly. "Thank you for coming."

"Thanks for having us. I see you're taking good care of Angelia," Claudia said.

"I'm trying."

"You better 'cause we don't want to have to cut you," Erica threatened with a half-smile.

Next on the list were Mrs. Holley and Miss Earlene, whom Amber insisted we invite. "Mom, she's like the grandma I never had."

"Okay, she can come," I had relented. Since a few weeks ago the woman had found a way for me to have enough time to get to the gym and have some sanity for two hours every night, thanks to Vacation Bible School, I couldn't say no.

"Nice to meet you" flowed from each guest.

The only person who seemed out of place—because she was—was Marcy. She was sitting alone at the end of a table with a glass of wine in hand. She'd said that the twins couldn't stay long, so she would stay for the food. I wasn't going to argue with her about not leaving the twins, so I gladly fixed her a plate. My cousins were civil with her, too.

The twins were sitting on the rocky platform just in front of the flowerbed in our back yard. They'd met my cousins at the wedding last year. "Y'all remember Claudia and Erica, right?"

"No," Tyler sassed without even looking up from her cell phone screen.

"Uh!" Claudia's left hand snatched the phone out of Tyler's hand before I could intervene. "Little girl, when there's a grown-up talking to you, you stop what you're doing and *acknowledge* them."

Tyler reached for the phone. Claudia quickly hid that left arm behind her back. Her right hand was inches away from Tyler's throat. Lord knows I wanted to watch the train-wreck happen because I'd wanted to snatch Tyler up a few times myself. However, this wasn't the time or the place.

I intervened, "Claudia, it's okay. Give it—"

"What's going on?" Marcy appeared out of nowhere.

"She took my phone!"

"I sure did because she was being very disrespectful and rude!" Claudia's neck was swiveling on its hinge as she explained herself to Marcy with no apology.

Marcy's hand went behind Claudia's back and I knew right then and there it was on.

"Don't touch me!"

"Don't touch what doesn't belong to you!" Marcy retorted.

"Maybe if you took care of what does belong to you, she wouldn't be so ghetto!" Erica jumped in.

My other guests had begun to take notice, sitting up in their chairs and straining their necks to get a look at the commotion.

"Stop it," I growled lowly. "This is more than just a family gathering. It's very important for Darren to impress his co-workers. Do *not* mess this up for him."

Thankfully, everyone in the circle had a vested interest in Darren's success.

Claudia gave the phone to me. I gave the phone to Tyler.

"We're leaving," Marcy said.

"Bye, Felicia," from Erica.

"Don't make me pull out *all* that weave in front of these white people."

"Go for it. It's one of you and five of us. You tell me which one of us gon' leave here trackless."

Marcy rolled her eyes and hightailed it to the side gate with Skylar and Tyler following close behind.

Their exit seemed to prompt the rest of our guests that it was time to leave.

"No, no need to leave," Darren tried to stop them.

One-by-one, they all made excuses. Coach Minden said it was getting late, Coach Bashlew said he had to get up early the next day. When it was clear that we couldn't convince them Marcy wasn't coming back to finish what my cousins kind of started, Darren, Mother Holley, and I tried to compensate by offering them plates of food to take with them.

They graciously accepted, but the fear in their eyes spoke volumes.

This is terrible!

Miss Earlene offered to stay and help me clean up but, honestly, I was too embarrassed. "That's sweet of you, but no, thank you. I've got plenty of hands around here to help."

"This is true." She nodded graciously.

At that point, only Mother Holley and Darren were left in the kitchen. I'd walked Demarcus upstairs and started his bath water. I stopped on the upstairs breezeway when I got a glimpse of Mother Holley poking Darren just as I had done when he first told me about these barbecue plans.

I stepped back into the shadows of the hallway and listened as she said to my husband, "See. I told you. Marry somebody with a jacked up past, you gonna have a jacked up future."

"Momma, Angelia is—"

"On her *third* husband. *Third.* A woman don't make it to her *third* husband unless there's something seriously wrong with her or she done figured out how to kill a man and get away with it."

I heard my husband sigh. "Goodnight, Momma."

Goodnight? Goodnight! Is that all he has to say? Goodnight!

He'd better be glad Claudia and Erica left with the rest of the crowd or they'd have him hemmed up in the corner by the refrigerator. I wanted to hem him up, myself, but what good would it do? If he wasn't willing to stand up for me on his own ... *it is what it is.*

Chapter 8

I woke up excited about my interview at Adkins Communications. When Ms. Startling called to set up my interview for the customer service position I was ecstatic. If hired, I would be part of a team of fifteen people giving 411 information to cell phone users. The calls would range from people needing phone numbers, movie times, flight information, dinner reservations, etc. This sector would be all-new to me but at this point that didn't matter. Customer service was customer service. I'd been on four interviews so something had to give.

I logged into my Facebook account to waste a little time. I had a few minutes to spare before leaving for my interview. My heart raced like crazy when I saw a message from Sherman. Sherman Johnson was my high school sweetheart and boy was I crazy about him.

Sherman and I dated from freshman year to my senior year. Sherman's two years older than me so he graduated before me. Sherman graduated and left for the Navy promising to send for me. We wrote each other every day and when he came home from boot camp he proposed to me, and I accepted; that was my sophomore year.

My cousins Erica and Claudia told me that I was crazy for wanting to be tied down to one man. Erica said that all military men are dogs and that Sherman would never be faithful to me. One evening I called Sherman but didn't get an answer;

Claudia was convinced that he was with another girl. Three days went by and he finally called me back stating that he was on watch duty unable to use the phone. Erica's words rang in my ear so I broke up with Sherman. Sherman tried to contact me, but I wouldn't respond.

I wonder what he could possibly want, especially since he's married to Tameka. Just the thought of him being with her made me sick to my stomach.

I clicked on my inbox and braced myself as I prepared to read the message.

"Hello, Angelia, I hope you're well. I ran across your profile and figured I'd give you a shout out. I live in Elk Manor, which is a 45-minute drive from Lancing Springs. Hit me up sometime and maybe we can meet up and have dinner or something."

I sat there staring at my screen. I read the message again, wondering what it all meant. What a coincidence it was that he lived in Elk Manor and my job interview was in Elk Manor.

I rushed out the door so that I could arrive to my interview on time.

I arrived at Adkins Communications and noticed that there were at least 20 people waiting to be seen. Surely the people waiting weren't applying for the same job I was interviewing for. I had on my black pantsuit that I'd purchased at Lord & Taylor and felt overdressed because everyone present looked as if they were just making a run to Wal-Mart Neighborhood Market. There was a girl with skinny jeans on, stilettos, a shirt with the word Boss on it with one of the letters barely hanging on it, probably her club clothes. I felt confident ... this job was mine. I strolled to the front desk and gave the receptionist my name and found a seat over in the far corner.

After waiting for 20 minutes the receptionist called me to go to the back for my interview.

A short, chubby man named Mr. Mitchell invited me into a cubicle that he referred to as an office for my interview. Mr. Mitchell looked over my resume checking and circling things with his red pen and finally looked up at me.

"Angelia, tell me why we should hire you?" he asked.

I wasn't prepared for that question and I guess he could tell from the look on my face.

"I have several years of experience and feel that I'm qualified for the position," I said.

"Angelia, from looking at your resume I see that you are overqualified; this is an entry level position. Not supervisory, like your previous job. Often, it's hard to step down and—"

"Mr. Mitchell, I really want this job," I said, literally begging him with my hands clasped together.

"I'm sorry Angelia, and I wish you well with your job search," he said, dismissing me.

I got up from the chair in disbelief. I rushed down the hallway and ran into Miss Skinny Jeans who had interviewed with another representative. I saw her with paperwork in her hand, I overheard the receptionist giving her directions to the nearest CareNow so that she could take her drug test. I almost ran to my car. I couldn't believe it; they probably hired ole girl because she's younger. Maybe I should've dressed like a pole dancer too.

On the drive home I cried so much that my eyes were puffy. Maybe moving here was a mistake. *My marriage is taking a turn for the worse; I'm not even sure if my husband still loves me. I still can't believe he didn't take up for me when he was talking to Mother Holley. Darren has allowed this move to change him. The only good thing about moving out here is me having my dream home.*

I pulled into my driveway and just sat in the car looking at the house. As beautiful as it was, I didn't feel like going in because Darren wasn't home. *I didn't get married to remain a single mom.*

I sighed and grabbed my purse to head in the house.

"Angelia, come here for a minute," Miss Earlene yelled from the porch.

I wasn't in the mood nor did I feel like being bothered but I crossed the green span over to her property anyway.

"I been meaning to invite you to our Tuesday night Women's Prayer and Bible study. It's for women of all ages, so you'll fit in just fine."

"Miss Earlene, thanks but no thanks. I'm not interested."

"Chile, how you know you ain't interested if you ain't never been? This group is going to help you with everything you been going through."

"I'm not going through anything; I'm fine," I said and before I knew it I was in tears.

"Come on inside and let's talk." Miss Earlene put her arm around me and ushered me into her living room.

Blinking away the tears I went inside.

"Talk to me Angelia, I know somethings wrong. I saw you sitting in your car loooking worried, and I know worried when I see it."

"Angelia, it's okay to cry, even Jesus wept. You can't keep goin' 'round pretending to be alright, pretending to be strong. Chile, you gotta learn how to take your burdens to the Lord, pray about 'em, and leave 'em there."

"I'm not so sure that God would even hear my prayer," I sobbed.

"Sho' He hears you, God knows all and sees all. You can't 'spect Him to help if you don't give Him a try. You should come tonight. You'll leave feeling better than when you came. Sandra Jean is picking me up and you can ride with us if you want to."

"No, I'll drive myself," I heard myself saying.

"Angelia, baby, God got you; it's going to be alright. Matter of fact, it's already alright, 'cause the God we serve won't fail."

I stood up, and Miss Earlene hugged me. I cried in her arms.

"That's it, chile, release it. Let go and let God."

I left Ms. Earlene's house feeling a little better. When I walked in the house Demarcus and Amber were playing a game on their Ps3.

"Hey Mom, how did the interview go?" Amber asked.

"I didn't get the job; they

said I was overqualified," I said, trying not to show my disappointment.

"That's okay, Mom. You'll find something better than that job," Amber encouraged me.

"Has Darren been home ... has he called?" I asked, knowing the answer.

"He called and said he would be late, said he should be home by 8:00."

"Okay, well tonight I won't be here, so find some pizza coupons and order pizza for you and your brother.'

"Mom, are you okay?" Demarcus asked.

"Baby, I'm fine," I said, hugging him, trying to reassure him.

"Why is Dad always gone? Why won't he spend any time with us?" Demarcus asked, sounding hurt.

"Your dad has to get use to his new job. Things will change soon, I promise," I said, not knowing if I believed what I said myself.

"Mom, where are you going?" Amber asked.

"I'm going to church with Miss Earlene."

"Really? That's awesome; I'm sure you'll enjoy it. I enjoyed going to Vacation Bible School with her. I wish we could join her church and go every Sunday," Amber said, sounding excited.

"Well, we'll see," I said.

I smiled and left the room before Amber saw the disappointment in my eyes. Darren hadn't called or texted me all day. I knew his reason for calling Amber and telling her about his late arrival was because he didn't want to hear my mouth.

I was sick of this, something had to give and soon. I knew it had always been his dream to be a coach but was it worth ruining his family over? I didn't know what would become of us. I loved my husband, I wanted my marriage to work. I desperately needed to clear my mind.

I went upstairs to find me something appropriate to wear to this Women's Prayer and Bible Study. I hadn't been to church in years and hadn't really missed it nor did I have a desire to go. I didn't know why, but for some reason I felt like I needed to go tonight, after all—I had nothing to lose.

Chapter 9

I walked inside of Mighty Movement of God Worship Center not really knowing why I decided to come. I hoped that my attire was satisfactory. After going through all of my clothes, I decided on a long black maxi skirt, my NeNe Leakes knit top with a sheer overlay and a pair of black wedge shoes. I walked slowly to the front door trying to decide if this was really what I wanted to do. Just as I was about to turn and go back to my car, Miss Earlene spotted me.

"Hey, Angelia I am so glad you came, this is Sandra Jean," she said, smiling.

"Nice meeting you," I said and shook her hand.

"It's good meeting you too. Miss Earlene talks about you all the time," Sandra Jean replied.

Sandra Jean looked to be in her mid-forties, but she dressed like she was Miss Earlene's age. Poor thing had on a long denim skirt, a shirt with a patch of flowers on the front of it and some nursing shoes.

"Y'all come on. Let's go, 'cause I don't want us to miss the opening prayer." Miss Earlene rushed down the hallway and Sandra Jean and I followed her.

When we arrived inside of the room there were 25 other women sitting in a circle of chairs. Miss Earlene told everyone I had come to observe. I was so glad she let it be known that I was there strictly to watch and listen, that's it and that's all.

"Good evening, ladies. What a blessing it is for us to be together one more time. Thank you for joining us this evening, Angelia. I'm Sister Dottie Hall, president of this women's group. It's our prayer that something that we say will be encouraging, inspiring and motivating to you."

I smiled and nodded my head.

"Tonight we're having open discussion. This is your opportunity to seek Godly advice from your sisters in Christ. We'll split up into our small groups and all of our seasoned saints will be in another room," Sister Dottie announced as Ms. Earlene and a few other ladies left the room. I really wanted to jump up and leave as well. She didn't inform me that I would be here by myself with total strangers. I felt my face getting hot.

"Hey, I'm Sheila. It's going to be alright," she encouraged me. "You look like you're about to pass out."

"This is all new to me, so I feel a little out of place," I admitted.

"Trust me, I did too when I first came, but now I love it. I've been here for six months."

"Alright, the question of the night is how do you handle feeling inadequate in your marriage. Do I have any volunteers who would like to share their thoughts on this?" Sister Dottie asked.

I shifted in my chair after hearing the topic. At first I was a little uncomfortable but was dying to hear the answers to the question.

Sheila raised her hand to be acknowledged to speak. "Praise the Lord, sisters. My name is Sheila Britt and I have been in this situation before. My husband, Frank got promoted to district manager on his job and I felt as if he had forgot about me. I was cooking, cleaning, running errands, doing everything that I needed to do around the house, as well as with the children, but still felt inadequate. I felt as if Frank was living in a new world without me.

"One evening I felt so down and out that one of my coworkers noticed my sadness and gave me a book to read. I figured I had nothing to lose so why not read it. The name of the book is *The Power of a Praying Wife* by Stormie Omartian. I began to read the book and it helped me a lot. I realized that my sufficiency is in God; only God can make me feel whole. Yes, I needed my husband but I needed God first to help me cope with Frank being absent from our marriage. I fasted and prayed for us as husband and wife, then I prayed for me and him individually. I asked God to restore our marriage, asked Him to fix me first.

"God began to change me and work on me. Oh what a wonderful change He's made in my life. Oh Hallelujah! And when I tell you God turned things around for us, He did. Thank you, Jesus. Lord, you're just so good. Glory to your Holy name. I started going to church more, start studying the word more, started trusting God more and Frank became a totally different person. I encourage you, my sister—whoever you are—to just hold to God's unchanging, never failing hand.

Give it to God and don't take it back. Prayer still works, y'all; I'm a living witness."

All of the ladies chimed in with giving God praise and I sat there silent, with tears running down my face. I was feeling numb because Sheila was telling my story. I needed to get a copy of that book, so that I could get my marriage fixed. I was going to make it a point to quiz Sheila on how things changed with her and Frank. The time went by fast after Sheila's testimony. Sister Dottie dismissed us in prayer and announced that the following week there would be Bible study and a spread.

"So do you think you'll come again?" Sheila asked.

"I'm not really sure, but I do want to get a copy of that book for a friend of mine," I said, not wanting her to know it was really for me.

"There's a Barnes and Noble on Conner St. I'm sure you can get your ... ummm, friend a copy there," Sheila said, letting me know that she didn't believe I was getting it for a friend.

"Thanks for the information. I'm sure it'll be helpful, I mean . . . I'm sure it'll help my friend."

"Angelia, I don't know you and you don't know me, but what I do know is that God was dealing with you tonight too. Here's my number. Call me if you need to talk . . . I am my sister's keeper," Sheila said, and handed me one of her business cards.

"Thanks," I said, and headed to my car.

I rode home in silence feeling hopeful. First thing tomorrow morning I was going to get a copy of that book. I pulled into my driveway, excited that Darren's car was in the driveway. Things were already looking better. I parked crazy and ran into the house and up the stairs only to find Darren in bed asleep. I couldn't believe he was asleep—it was only 8:45p.m.

My phone dinged to let me know I had a message. I went into the hallway to see who would be trying to contact me, thinking it was probably Erica or Claudia. I opened my phone and saw a Facebook message from Sherman.

Hey Angelia, call me when you get a chance. I'd like to chat and catch up. Here's my number. Hope to hear from you soon.

My hand was shaking so hard, I almost dropped my phone. I went back downstairs and sat in my recliner, debating if I should call him. Both kids were upstairs in their rooms but as large as the house is it's easy for someone to sneak up on you. With Darren asleep, he obviously didn't care one way or the other if I'd arrived home safely, but there was still a possibility he'd come looking for me if he looked outside and saw my car.

I grabbed my phone and headed outside to the car. I could make the call from there and if for some reason Darren came outside, I could end the call and just say it was Erica or Claudia. I dialed the number and let the phone ring twice. Then hung up. What was I doing? My hands were sweating. I wondered what Sherman wanted. Did he want to get back together? Had he been thinking about me? Why was I thinking about that? *I'm married.* The phone rang and scared me so, I almost jumped out of my skin. It was Sherman calling me back.

"Hello," I said, trying to sound calm.

"Angelia, is this you?"

"Um ... yeah, it's me; how did you know?"

"Wishful thinking. How've you been?"

"All is well, how are you and Tameka doing?"

"I'm fine and I guess Tameka's okay too; we're divorced."

I have no idea why I was glad to hear that he was no longer with her.

"I'm sorry to hear that," I said with a huge smile on my face.

"I'd really like for us to get together and catch up, you know, face to face. What's your schedule like for tomorrow? Maybe we can go to Mr. Gatti's and grab a pizza."

"Mr. Gatti's? Wow, I haven't been there in years. I can't believe you still go there," I said, shocked that he remembered our old hangout. Sherman and I used to go to Mr. Gatti's almost every weekend; it was our special place. I couldn't believe all these years later he would still remember that. *Ummph.* Darren couldn't tell me what I fixed for dinner last night if I asked him.

"Why wouldn't I? I still love their pizza and I figured you still do too, so why not just meet there? You know we can reminisce about the good ole days, or we can go somewhere else if you'd like."

"No that's fine, pizza is fine with me.

"Okay cool. They've got a Mr. Gatti's inside the Elk Manor Mall. I'll meet you there at 1:30 p.m. tomorrow. Have a good night, Angelia, and I look forward to seeing you tomorrow."

"Okay, sounds good. You have a good night as well," I said, hanging up the phone.

I sat in the car trying to digest everything. I was having lunch with Sherman Johnson tomorrow. I needed to find a beautician, buy a new outfit, and get my nails and feet done. In the words of my favorite reality TV star, Tamar Braxton, "I need to be snatched." I got out of the car humming and feeling excited until I felt someone watching me. Miss. Earlene was standing on the porch looking at me as if she could see right through me. I knew she couldn't have heard my conversation because I had the window up but something about the way she looked at me made me feel eerie, so I waved and went inside of the house.

Chapter 10

"Angelia, babe, today I should be home early. This is the last week of the two-a-day practices, so hopefully I can make it home early today. Our first game is next week," Darren said as he prepared to leave.

"Oh, okay that's fine," I said nonchalantly.

I guess he was expecting a different response, but I was sick of his broken promises and refused to hype myself up again for a big letdown. I love Darren, but it was time for him to show me that he loves me too.

"Angelia, I know you're upset about me being asleep last night, but—"

"But you were tired, I know," I said, cutting him off.

Darren went into the bathroom and finished getting ready. I was ready for him to leave so that I could go to Unique Hair & Nail Spa to get hooked up. I read online that it was an upscale salon. The guy who owned the shop reminded me of Derek J from the reality show *The Real Housewives of Atlanta.* Although I didn't have an appointment, I was hoping that he could squeeze me in.

"Alright babe, I'll see you later," Darren said and gave me a quick peck.

"Okay, have a good one."

Darren left and I ran into the closet to find me something to throw on. It was 7:00 a.m. and I needed to get to the salon and I still needed to get an outfit to wear as well. I threw on a sundress that I picked up from Ross, a baseball cap and a pair of sandals. Normally I wouldn't go anywhere looking like this, but I was on a mission and the end result would be that I would look fabulous.

I went into the kitchen and left a note for Amber to make sure she fixed breakfast and lunch for Demarcus. I told her I would be out job hunting most of the day. I hated lying, but what was I supposed to say... *I'm meeting the man who should've been your daddy for lunch?*

When I entered the salon it was crowded, but I was determined to get my hair done.

I walked up to the receptionist and told her I needed someone who specialized in cutting and coloring hair. I decided since it was summer I wanted something fierce, a fiery red-hot color. I signed in and waited for my name to be called.

"Mrs. Holley, Zeke is ready for you," the receptionist informed me.

I followed her to Zeke's station and he had pictures of himself with different clients showcasing their various looks. I saw a picture of a girl with a short, edgy bob; although it was a little outside of the box for me, I made up my mind that was what I wanted.

"Hello darling, I'm Zeke and I'll be your stylist for today," he said proudly.

"I'm Angelia Holley, it's nice to meet you, Zeke."

"Alright, take a seat and let me see what we're working with," Zeke said, taking my baseball cap off of my head.

"Oh my. I see it's been a while since you've been to a salon." He poked through my hair with a rat-tail comb, examining my split ends and uneven layers. "What did you have in mind for today?"

"I want to get my hair cut in a bob like the lady in the picture, but I want to add some color; I want a fiery red color," I said.

"Honey, if you get that red, you gotta have that attitude to go with it," Zeke's co-worker shouted from across the room.

"Ignore Paul, he always has something to say. Anyway, have you ever had permanent color on your hair before?" Zeke asked.

"No, I've only had a rinse."

"Okay great. Let me grab the color and a cape and we'll get started. I'm going to cut your hair first," Zeke said, and went to go fetch his supplies.

After a 2 1/2 hour process, I was ready to see the finished product.

"OMG I love it, I love it! I absolutely love it!" I shouted.

"I aim to please, hun, and you look gorgeous, darling if I must say so myself," Zeke bragged.

"Yeah, you working that do," Paul chimed in.

"Oh I forgot … I need to get my nails and feet done as well," I said.

"Whatcha getting ready for or shall I say *who* you getting ready for?" Paul asked.

"Paul, stay out of people's business. I want Ms. Angelia to come back again, but dang, you about to run her off," Zeke said, sounding irritated.

I laughed and ignored Paul.

"So Zeke, what do I need to do next?" I asked.

"Follow me and we'll get you taken care of," Zeke said.

"Alright, Ms. Angelia, I'll see you next time, and I still say you ain't fooling nobody, hun. I can see it in your face," Paul said.

Paul was really making me nervous...Was I really looking some kinda way? I waved at him and followed Zeke.

By the time I finished getting my nails and feet done, it was 11:00 a.m. I needed to run to Macy's and pick up a cute outfit. I didn't have a whole bunch of time, 'cuz I was scheduled to meet Sherman at 1:30 p.m. When I made it to Macy's, I saw Coach Minden's wife and decided to hide in a dressing room until she left. *Oh boy, that was a close call.* The last thing I needed was for her to go back and report that she saw me in Macy's. That would mess up my job-hunting lie.

I found a cute tiger print jumper with single-sole sandals that had glittery-gold, with sexy straps winding up my ankle and legs *Haute.* I topped off the outfit with some gold accessories to match. I couldn't go back home to change, so I paid for the outfit and changed in the bathroom, did my makeup too. I was pushed for time and needed to hit the road for Elk Manor.

A New Beginning

I got in the car and admired my new look. I was fierce to the max and feeling good too.

I turned on my radio. They were playing Fantasia's "Truth Is." I hadn't heard the song but a couple of times, but it certainly reminded me of the good ole days with Sherman. We used to have so much fun laughing, talking, and just hanging out. Sherman wasn't just my boyfriend, he was my friend, too. I screwed up when I let him get away. *I wonder how things would have been with us. I probably wouldn't be going through half the mess I'm going through now if I would've stayed with him.* I made it to Elk Manor in no time. I found the mall and had five minutes to spare. I waited five additional minutes before going inside to find Mr. Gatti's, because I wanted to make an entrance.

Just as I was getting out of the car my phone rang and it was Darren. I pressed the ignore button and walked inside to find Sherman.

I looked around and spotted him waving for me to join him. I walked over to the table, head high and confident.

"Angelia, *wow* you look amazingly beautiful, and I love your hair," Sherman said, hugging me and giving me a peck on the cheek.

"You don't look bad yourself," I said, taking a deep breath, and thinking, *Why does he have to smell so good?*

Sherman pulled my chair out for me to sit down. That's Sherman … always a gentleman. Good Lord, he was still handsome as ever: tall, Idris Elba look alike, can you say chocolaty? Oooooooweeeeeee,

91

this man was still fine. I loved to see a man in a nice suit. Sherman had on a nice black and grey pinstripe suit, with a pink shirt and a pink, gray and white tie. I felt my temperature rising.

"I figured you wouldn't want to do the buffet, so I ordered your favorite: pepperoni, jalapeno pepper, black olive and mushroom, right?" Sherman asked with a twinkle in his eye.

Is he flirting? "Yes," I said, too mesmerized to say more.

My phone dinged to let me know I had received a text message. It was Amber. I read the message:

"Mom where are you? Dad is home, said he tried to call you."

"Is that something you need to take care of?" Sherman asked, concerned.

"Oh no, it's ok, just someone from my Bible study group needing to ask a question," I said. *I can't believe how easily that lie slipped off my tongue.*

The pizza arrived and Sherman blessed the food.

"Oooo, this looks good; I haven't had this pizza in years," I said.

We both got a couple of slices of pizza and dug in.

"Angelia, the reason I wanted us to meet is so that I can apologize to you," Sherman said, wiping his mouth with a napkin.

"Apologize for what?"

"I was young and foolish; I shouldn't have given up on us so soon," Sherman said.

"I broke up with you based on what Erica and Claudia said. We were both young and didn't know any better, so I apologize, too."

"I'm glad that you agreed to meet with me because that's been bothering me for quite some time now. I often wonder how things would have been between us, but I am glad to know you're doing well now. I saw pictures of you and your family on Facebook and you and your husband look like a happily married couple," Sherman said, taking a swig of Pepsi.

My phone dinged again. This time the message was from Darren.

"Ugh," I groaned aloud and read the message.

"Babe, I know you're angry but please call me back. I'm home. Let me make it up to you. Love you."

"Are you sure everything's ok?" Sherman asked.

"Yeah it's all good. Now where were we?"

"I was just saying that I'm glad you and your husband are doing great and I hope that he's okay with us being friends. You did tell him we were meeting today, right?"

"Of course I told him." I had no intentions of ever mentioning Sherman to Darren.

"Good, because I don't want to interfere in your marriage."

"So what happened with you and Tameka?"

"Well for starters, we shouldn't have gotten married; we didn't really know each other as well as we should have." Sherman said.

"So why did you marry her?"

"I married her because I honestly loved her, but she wasn't in love me. Long story short, Tameka wasn't ready to settle down. Marrying someone because they're pregnant is not the best thing to do. We were young and allowed others to talk us into getting married when clearly we weren't ready. I hate it took us having two children before we figured it out. We both agreed that we should divorce and now we're the best of friends for the sake of the children. It's not something that I'm proud of," Sherman said, clearing his throat.

"How did you come to that realization?" I asked.

"There were times when Tameka would go out with her friends and wouldn't come home. I would be home with our sons. I would suggest that we go out together, but she always had an excuse why she couldn't. Tameka's friends were single and ready to help her mingle. I needed her home with my sons and me but she wasn't there.

"One day my brother, Alex, called me and told me that Tameka's car was parked at the Holiday Inn Express. I didn't want to believe him, but I drove there and sure enough, it was her. She ended up pregnant and although she had a miscarriage, I couldn't trust her. I believe in marriage and in the marriage covenant and what it stands for and I tried to get past it, but just couldn't. We got a divorce and as we were going through the divorce, I got a job here. My boys live with her and we alternate weekends and holidays."

"I'm sorry she did that to you, Sherman."

"Well you live and you learn. I believe everything happens for a reason and I know God has a purpose and a plan for our lives. We just have to learn to trust and obey God and wait on Him. That's the problem. We want a quick fix, want what we want and we take too much stuff for granted."

"So are you *Pastor* Johnson now?" I asked jokingly.

"No, but I am a deacon at my church and have been for three years now. God has truly changed my life, Angelia. What's the name of your church and how long have you been there?" Sherman asked.

"Well you know we just moved to Lancing Springs, so right now I'm attending The Mighty Miracle Movement of God church," I said, hoping Sherman wasn't familiar with the church because then he'd know I was telling another lie … well, it wasn't really a lie. I did attend yesterday.

"Good for you, it's important for the family to have a strong foundation and that foundation has to be Jesus Christ. There's no way we can make it without Him, Amen?" Sherman said, finishing up his sermonette.

"Amen," I chimed in, feeling uneasy.

The phone rang again and this time it was Sherman's phone.

"Excuse me, I've got to take this call," he said and left the table.

A few minutes went by and Sherman returned.

"Angelia, it was good seeing you, but I've got to go. That was Tameka … my youngest son, Bradley fell off of a slide and broke his arm. They're at the hospital now. I've already paid the bill. Hopefully we can get together again," Sherman said.

"Oh okay. Yeah, go ahead; I totally understand," I said.

Sherman rushed out of the door. I sat there for a minute feeling dumb. I went out of my way for a man who was clearly over me. *Why did I do this? What was I really expecting from Sherman? What's happening to me?* I left and went to my car feeling lost, confused and ashamed of myself.

Chapter 11

Sherman Johnson. Bible-thumpin', born-again believer. Who would have thought? On my way back to Lancing Springs, my emotions traveled the length of two runaway rollercoasters. *Was he leading me on?*

I mentally replayed our phone conversation. Sherman had said he wanted to "catch up." *Catch up.* When I thought about it, I realized I had taken "catch up" to mean "pick up where we left off."

How stupid can I be? I had single-handedly managed to get dismissed from employment, tell three lies, and get my face broken in front of my ex-boyfriend in less than twenty-four hours.

This is ridiculous. Sherman didn't want me. Adkins didn't want me. And at the rate Darren and I were going, he obviously wouldn't want me, either.

I should have known my good luck streak wasn't going to last forever. Sooner or later, life always slapped me back down to reality. Who was I kidding? I was just a little black girl from Marshall, TX. I finished high school but promptly dropped out of Wiley College when I met, fell in love with, and ran to the Justice of the Peace's office to marry Javar. He'd convinced me to move to Dallas with him. *Stupid. Stupid. Stupid.*

Little did I know, he was just trying to move his hustle to a bigger city. That's why he got shot and sent to prison. Trying to live the thug life.

My second husband was a womanizer with terrible credit. And there I was living off of my third husband like a common prostitute, except we really weren't having much sex.

Maybe Mother Holley was right. People like Darren, who had grown up in good two-parent homes, were in a different class than me. They were stable. They were lucky. Good things just *happened* to them. Except for his misjudgment of Marcy, Darren had caught all the breaks.

Until he met me. Not only was I dead weight in his life with my two kids, I had actually considered cheating on him with Sherman. *What kind of person am I?*

I didn't deserve Darren. I needed to end this relationship now. We hadn't been married long. Maybe we could get an annulment.

I didn't deserve a nice, calm family in a big ol' house in the suburbs. I made up my mind then and there on the ride back home that it was time for me to put an end to this farce. The writing had been on the wall since we'd moved to Lancing Springs a month earlier. Who was I kidding anyway? We had only dated less than a year before getting engaged. We'd moved too quickly. Real love doesn't work that way. Darren was better off without me. Maybe they'd all be better off without me.

Amber was pretty much grown. She'd be leaving for college soon. Amber had always been a self-sufficient child. Never had much use for me anyway.

As much as I hated to consider letting Demarcus move with

his father, maybe Marcus could do a better job than me since all I was doing was shuffling them from place-to-place. I saw once on a National Geographic documentary that young lions need an alpha male in their lives or they would never learn how to respect authority. Granted, people aren't lions, but still. I didn't want Demarcus to end up a statistic like me.

As for myself, it was time to … to start over. To go somewhere far away where no one knew me and just be. With no Miss Earlenes trying to save my soul. No Darrens trying to make me seem normal, and no Mother Holleys to point out the painful truth. I drove around trying to get my thoughts together. I didn't realize how beautiful Lancing Springs really is with its rolling hills and . An hour later I decided to head home.

I wasn't expecting to see Darren's car in the driveway. Getting Amber and Demarcus packed up and ready to leave would have been a lot easier without Darren there. After all, being raised by a working-class single mom, my kids had experienced a 24-hour eviction notice or two over the years.

I took a deep breath, put on my survivalist game face, and marched into the house. No need to raise the garage—I didn't want Darren to trap me inside. Instead, I traipsed to the front door, opened it, but stopped short at the sight of the huge crack in the star in my tiled floor. "Who did this!" I yelled like it really mattered what happened to the house at that point.

"Babe," Darren called from his office down the side hallway. "Come here. I need to talk to you."

"Who broke the entryway floor?" I yelled at no one in particular.

"My suitcase did it," I heard from a voice that sent anger gushing through my veins.

The twins are here. And they're tearing up my house in more ways than one. Actually, the fact that they had torn up my tile was perfect. Darren could have this house and those disrespectful girls of his.

"Babe!" from my husband again.

No time like the present to tell him it's over. I stomped down the hallway, determined to display the stankiest, most unattractive attitude possible so that Darren would see the light.

He was sitting at his desk with his hands folded under his chin. He glanced up at me. From the way he looked up and down, he clearly recognized a difference in my appearance. Yet, he gave no compliment. Only a somber expression. "Baby, sit down. I need to talk to you."

I barely tapped my rear end on the edge of the leather office chair across from his desk. "I already know, Darren. It's not going to work out between the two of us."

"What?"

"You made a mistake marrying me. I made a mistake marrying a man who wanted a replacement mother for his children and who loves football more than me. I agree, we should cut our losses."

"Angelia, what are you talking about?"

I stood and planted an index finger on the mahogany desk. If this was going to be our last conversation, I wanted to let it all out. "Don't patronize me. And while I'm at it, let's talk

100

about your mother. She might be right about me, but *you* should have put her in check. Just like you should have put Marcy in check. You put *everyone* in a terrible position by not being here and not drawing boundaries. I hope you've learned your lesson so you can be ready for *your* third wife."

I turned quickly on the heel of my new slinky shoes I'd bought to impress Sherman. Too quickly. My foot slipped on the slick padding. Those brand new straps were merciless. Before I knew it, I was flat on the floor with my left ankle twisted some kind of way.

"Angelia!" Darren rushed to my side.

"I'm okay." Lie number four for the day. My ankle felt like a pit bull had just taken a chunk out of my flesh. So much for shock-delay, I was in full-on pain.

He tried to help me up, but I knew if I got anywhere near putting weight on that ankle, I would faint. "Leave me alone." On hands and knees, I tried to crawl out of his office. "I'm leaving."

He stayed down with me, "Baby, what's come over you? I need to talk to you—but not about leaving. What's—"

If I could have gnawed off my foot like a rabbit I would've. The physical pain mixed with my emotional turmoil and the fact that my husband and I were both on the floor crawling down the hallway brought tears to my eyes. I screamed like the wounded animal I was. "Just leave me and my kids alone!"

"Your kids are *my* kids. And vice versa. That's what I'm trying to tell you. The girls have to move here. I'm going to court to get them from Marcy."

Really, that was all I needed to hear. I crawled faster. "That's just great, Darren! You and your girls will love this freakin' house! Why don't you move Marcy in, too?"

"Don't be ridiculous." Darren reached for my hip.

I lunged forward. We both fell, with him on top of me.

"Get off! Get off of me!" I tried to sling my purse at him, but the effort nearly threw my shoulder out of whack.

"Angelia! Stop!"

I heard the telltale sound of Demarcus's feet racing down the staircase. I sat up against the skip-trowel textured walls, dragging my injured foot close to my behind, trying to make myself somewhat presentable before my baby saw this fiasco. He'd seen a lot of drama, but nothing like this foolishness.

Darren and I were both breathing heavily when Demarcus approached the hallway. "What's going on?"

"Nothing. We're talking," I said.

"Why are y'all on the floor?"

"Because your momma fell. Let's help her up."

"What's wrong with her hair?" my son asked.

"There's nothing wrong with my hair. It's just red."

"Oh."

Darren coached my son, "You grab her right side. I'll pull up her left."

On the count of three, they hoisted me to a standing position. The rush of blood sent an uncomfortable pressure to my ankle, which was already swelling.

Darren took a quick glance down as they guided me to the

family room couch. He elevated my ankle on a pillow and gently removed my shoe. "We need to get to an emergency room for x-rays."

"I can drive myself."

"No. You can't. I'm driving you."

"No. I'm not going anywhere with you."

"Then I'll call 9-1-1."

"I have someone else who can take me." I was up to four lies now.

A flash of jealousy crossed Darren's face. "Who?"

"Don't you worry about who. Shouldn't you be at football practice or a coaches' meeting?"

"There's a reason why I'm here. And a reason why the girls are here, too. I *need* to talk to you. Alone."

Demarcus's head swiveled back and forth, taking in an earful of grown-up business.

"I've needed you for several weeks. Didn't matter to you. Don't think I'm supposed to jump when you call. This is just … not going to work."

I pulled my wallet from my purse. "I'm going to call my friend now."

"Who is this friend?" he asked again.

"You don't know 'em."

"Demarcus, go to your room," Darren ordered.

I arrested my son's arm. "He doesn't have a room. We don't live here anymore. We'll be leaving as soon as I get back from CareNow, broken ankle or not."

"We're   leaving,

Momma?" Demarcus asked with sheer sadness on his little brown face. He slipped an arm around Darren's waist. Darren reciprocated with an arm across Demarcus's shoulder.

I wasn't prepared for the sight of the two most important men in my life standing in solidarity against my desire to run away from it all.

From the corner of my eye, I caught movement in the balcony. Amber was standing overhead. Watching. With the twins behind her. All of them wore the same expression as my son. Skylar and Tyler had seen it happen to Darren and Marcy. Demarcus and Amber had seen it happen to me and Marcus. And now, they were all watching the nightmare play out again as our family split up right before their very eyes.

Darren looked up at the girls. Then at me again.

What am I doing?

"I...I'm going to call my friend now."

The only "friend" who came to mind, the only person within forty-five minutes of Lancing Springs who might understand my dilemma without being judgmental, was Sheila.

Chapter 12

I wasn't sure if Sheila came to pick me up because she was a woman of her word or because I was boo-hooing like I needed a strait jacket. Nonetheless, I gave her my address and she rang my doorbell twenty minutes later.

Darren let her in the house. He and Sheila introduced themselves. "She's in there," he told her.

Sheila rushed to my side and knelt down beside the couch. "Honey, are you okay?"

I fell into her open arms. "I just need ... help."

She got a look at my ice-packed foot, then pulled me in for a tight hug again and whispered into my ear, "Did he do this to you?"

I backed away, wiping my face. "No. I fell. The shoes." I pointed at my discarded heel.

Sheila picked up my shoe, twirled it from left to right. "These are cute."

"Thank you."

Glad to know that she was a shoe-woman after my own heart, I said, "Let's go bond somewhere else."

She stared at my swollen ankle. "Like a hospital?"

"No. I'm too upset to go to a hospital right now."

"Well ... we could go to my house, since you really need to stay off that leg. My husband is out of town doing site visits for the stores in his territory. If you don't mind a Pomeranian and teenagers, you can spend the evening at my place. Sort things out. Pray."

"What's a Pomeranian?"

"A dog."

"How big is it?"

Sheila held one hand at her chest, the other at her waist.

"Okay. That's not too big. Let's go."

With her help, I got off the couch and into her Honda Accord. Darren brought a pair of crutches to the car.

"You can put them in the back seat, Darren," Sheila directed. "Thank you."

He followed her advice, then walked around to my side of the car. I supposed he was waiting for me to roll the window down, but I didn't want to hear anything he had to say so I sat there facing the windshield.

"Sis, your husband wants to speak to you."

"I know." I stared straight ahead.

"Don't you want to—"

"No."

To my dismay, Sheila used her driver's side control to lower my window.

Darren leaned in and kissed my cheek. "See you when you get home, baby."

I politely rolled the window back up without a reply.

Shelia overrode my effort, sending the window back down again. "We'll call you in a few hours. If her ankle gets much bigger, we'll meet you at the hospital."

"Thanks." Finally satisfied, he walked away.

I griped, "Whose side are you on anyway?"

"The Lord's."

Couldn't argue with that team. I sighed. "Let's roll."

With every bump and dip on the street, my leg bounced painfully on the floorboard. I tried to hold it up, but the weight of the extra fluid building made my attempts impossible. "Ouch!" and "Ooh!" escaped my mouth as the pressure in my ankle grew from keeping it below my heart.

Sheila asked me twice if I was okay.

"Yes."

And then we small-talked as she continued driving. Honestly, I didn't hear a word she was saying. I already knew I wasn't going to be able to concentrate again until I got on a couch, put another cool compress on my foot, and downed more than the recommended dosage of Advil.

Before I knew it, Sheila was pulling into the parking lot of a CareNow clinic. "Why are we here?"

"Angelia, you're hurt."

"No, I'm not. It's a sprain. Probably."

"I've listened to you moan and groan since you got in the car. Even if it is just a sprain, you need prescription-strength relief."

"Really?"

"Really."

I plopped my head against the headrest. "What have I gotten myself into with you?"

"A real friendship. A sisterhood. The kind where we tell each other what we *need* to hear. Come on. I'm not taking no for an answer."

She helped me out of the car and handed me the crutches, but they were too tall for my height. We threw them back in the car. Sheila allowed me to bear down on her shoulder as we maneuvered to the doors and up to the counter. We must have looked like a terrible three-legged race.

"Ouch!" I fussed.

"Scooch your hip over, girl!" she fussed back.

We had to laugh at ourselves.

By the time we signed in and sat down in the waiting area, I knew I had come across a rare find: Someone I could trust and lean on, literally.

There weren't many people waiting to be seen, which meant we only had a short wait before they called me back to a room. Sheila asked if I wanted her to come along.

"Sure."

Once in the small examination room, a nurse assistant asked me a few questions, recorded my responses, and said the doctor would be with me shortly.

"Thank you."

When she left, Sheila got to the nitty-gritty. "So. What's going on?"

I leaned back on the examination bench like someone pouring out my heart in a psychiatrist's office. "It's exactly what you said at church the other night. My husband is always gone. Always at work. He's a new football coach at Lancing Springs."

"What a blessing!"

"No, it's not. I mean, it is *financially*, but ... and then my stepdaughters! It's like he wants me to halfway raise them! And they're *bad*."

"Don't say that."

"Say what?" I asked.

"Kids aren't *bad*. Kids are *untrained*."

"Bad, untrained, whatever. I did not sign up to train two more children."

"But you knew he had kids, right?"

"Yes," I admitted.

"And both your kids live with you, right?"

"Yes, but he knew what he was getting into. I didn't know my husband's hidden agenda for moving to Lancing Springs. He dumped the girls on me when we moved here."

"Don't say that."

"Say what?"

"Dumped. They're not trash."

I rocked my head to the right and landed with my eyes locked on Sheila's. "Are you always this positive?"

"I'm more than positive. I'm full of the joy of the Lord, and that's what I want for you. I know it's hard when your husband isn't home. Been there and I'm doing that now." She rolled her neck. "My husband has a son from an *affair* who comes home from college every weekend he can. So you're preaching to the choir."

"An affair?!" I raised up on my elbows.

"Yes. An affair. Well,

technically, we were separated. And he got another woman pregnant while we were apart. Still, we were not divorced. But God. He restored our marriage and our love for each other."

I laid back down, shaking my head. "Sheila, girl, you're better than me."

"No, I'm not. I'm just a little further along down the road, looking back to tell you that your marriage can make it with the help of the Lord. You still love your husband, and he still loves you. It's all in the body language. "

I closed my lids, not wanting to validate the truth and betray my sense of entitlement to anger.

"You know what I think?" she asked.

"I've got a feeling you're going to tell me whether I want to hear it or not."

"No, I'll wait until you're ready."

I threw my hands up and let them fall down. "Go ahead."

"I think the Lord has blessed you with a wonderful man and *four* wonderful children. The week we had Vacation Bible School, I helped out with the older kids. Those twins have some smart mouths, but underneath that wanna-be-Sasha-Fierce attitude, they're really two sensitive girls. When we had anonymous-question night, I made note of their pen color. Both of them were using purple ink. I read their questions. I won't break my vow of confidence by telling you exactly what they wrote, but I can tell you, they are starving for attention. Starving for love. And if they don't get it from the right people, they'll soon get it from the wrong ones."

Lord knows I didn't want Skylar and Tyler to end up pregnant by age fifteen. That would make me a step-grandmother!

"Another thing. You don't think God blessed you with all those bedrooms in that wonderful house just so they can sit up and grow cobwebs, do you?"

"They're guest rooms," I said.

"But they're meant to be used, right?"

"For *guests*. Not live-ins."

Sheila rolled over on her stool. She placed her hand on my arm. "Angelia, I'm going to tell you what the Lord is speaking to my heart right now. I have to say this, so I'm not asking permission. You understand?"

"Yes."

"You're on assignment. You're a helpmate to your husband and a role model to his daughters as well as your kids. You need to *own* your role and not run from it. God is going to use your family, the extra rooms He has given you, and the model of your marriage to show His love even beyond the twins. He's giving you your testimony in this."

Oh no! I thought to myself. I didn't want a testimony. I didn't want to be used by God, nor did I want my stuff or my marriage to be used by Him. I wanted my life, my man, and my stuff for myself.

Good thing the doctor came into the room. He and an assistant led me to an x-ray room. When they were finished snapping images, the assistant asked if I wanted to go back and wait in my examination room.

"No. May I stay here until the results are available?"

"Sure," she said.

I didn't want to face Sheila alone again. I was afraid of her and almost angry with her at the same time. I tried to think of all the reasons to not receive her words. *Is her life perfect? Can't be. If it were so perfect, her husband wouldn't have a love child!*

But she'd said that was before God changed her marriage. If God changed her marriage, He had probably changed her, too. Maybe even her kids. Hopefully her husband—that cheatin'-machine.

Plus, I never really liked anyone who had a dog in their house anyway. That's nasty.

Still. The words she had spoken to me seemed to burn a hole in my heart. *The Lord wants to use me, my marriage, and even my home to help people?* The very thought that my life had a bigger purpose than me ... well, I really didn't know *what* to think.

The nurse interrupted my pondering with news that the x-ray showed that I hadn't broken anything. It was a severe sprain, as I suspected.

"That's great."

"The doctor wants you to stay off of it for a week. He's writing a few prescriptions for you, including crutches. You can have a seat in the main lobby until they're ready."

"Praise God," Sheila said when I met her again in the lobby and gave her the good news.

With a proper pair of crutches from the clinic, I was able to make it to her car on my own. Sheila put them on top of the other pair in the back seat while I settled in the front.

She hopped in. "I'm so glad it wasn't broken."

"Me, too. They've called in a prescription for pain and inflammation."

"Mmmm hmmm. You'll thank me tonight."

"I'll thank you *now*. I appreciate you being here for me."

"Any time. When I gave you that card, I meant for you to use it. Just like I meant everything else I said to you."

I nodded submissively, unable to refute anything. "I feel you."

"Okay. Where to?"

Her question gave me pause. She'd already given an invitation to go to her home. I could make Darren wait. Make him sweat. But, honestly, that would also make everyone else in the house sweat. I didn't want my kids or the *untrained* ones to suffer, too.

Even more importantly, I didn't want to hear any more of Sheila's preaching. Even if she was right.

"Take me home."

"You ain't said nothin' but a word."

Chapter 13

Sheila and I went to Walgreen's to pick up my prescription and headed to my house. I was feeling a little nervous. I guess I hadn't really thought about what would happen upon my arrival. What if Darren changed his mind about us and wanted us to leave? *I don't have any money and Lord knows I can't go back to Dallas to face my family, and of course, all of the haters who would love to see me fail.*

"Angelia, what's on your mind? You're quiet," Sheila said.

"Nothing, I'm just ready to get home and relax," I said, not wanting to share my thoughts with her. I'd already shared more than I had intended to.

"Things are going to work out; I know that's what you're worried about."

"How do you know?" I asked.

"I know because everything that we go through in life has reasoning behind it. I told you the other night at Bible study that God is dealing with you. Although you may not want to believe it, I see it. I was just like you, but once I gave my life to Christ and surrendered to Him, I changed. He changed my walk, my talk, my everything and I can tell that you want to change too," Sheila said matter of factly.

"Oh, so now you work with Dionne Warwick and her psychic friends hotline?" I asked, laughing.

"Hahaha. And are you one of the Queens of Comedy now?" Sheila said, getting me back.

"Whatchu know about that?"

"Oh, so you think just because I love the Lord and go to church I don't have fun?"

"Well every time I talk to you, you're talking about church or about the Lord. I thought that's all you did," I confessed.

"Angelia, I talk about the Lord because I love Him and because I know He's the one Who will help you through your trying times. Yes, I go to church faithfully, but I also like to go shopping, to the movies, out to eat, bowling, and to comedy shows. I love to have fun."

"I'm sorry, I thought all you did was read your Bible all day."

"Girl, you are something else, for real. It's so funny how people judge the church folks. Why don't you come to church so you can see how much fun we have. We have our Family and Friends Day and afterwards we play games and enjoy each other."

"I won't make any promises, but I'll think about it," I said.

We rode the rest of the way in silence. I guess there's more to Sheila than I expected. I probably wouldn't visit her house because of the dog situation, but I'd consider hanging out with her. LOL.

"Well here we are, your home sweet home." Sheila pulled into the driveway, went to ring my doorbell.

"What are you doing?" I yelled out of the window.

"I'm getting your husband

so that he can get you inside the house."

"I don't need his help," I said, grabbing my crutches out of the back seat. I attempted to balance myself, and reach my purse and before I knew it I fell.

"Angelia, babe, don't try to get up; I'll carry you." Darren ran to me and picked me up off of the ground.

"Girlfriend, you're one stubborn cookie. Call me if you need me; I'm headed home," Sheila announced.

"Thanks for everything. I owe you big time," Darren addressed Sheila.

"Yeah, thanks Sheila," I said with my head lowered. I was too embarrassed to even look her in the eye.

"You're both welcome; that's what friends are for. And Darren, you can repay me by being my guest for Family and Friends Day service in two weeks. I was telling Angelia about it on the way here."

"Okay, I'll keep that in mind. Thanks again," Darren said.

"Goodnight, y'all ... be blessed."

Sheila got in her car and drove off.

Darren carried me to the couch in our living room and sat me down. I was trying to read him but couldn't. I didn't know if he was going to put me out or what. Darren was pacing the floor; he was really making me feel uneasy.

"Angelia, babe, we really need to talk. I know you're in a lot of pain, but there's something we need to discuss tonight," Darren said, with a serious look on his face.

"I'll have my bags packed and my kids and I will be out of

here first thing in the morning." I blurted out, knowing I couldn't afford for us to leave, nor did I have a place for us to go.

"Babe, why in the world would you say that? Don't you know I love you? I love you, Amber and Demarcus and I can't imagine my life without you," Darren said, teary eyed.

"Well, you coulda fooled me, 'cause you've been living your life without me ever since we moved here," I said, with an attitude.

"You're right ... I haven't been here, and I apologize for it. I know I need to be here more. I was so caught up in making a good impression that I neglected you and our children. Coach Minden and I have been talking and he made me realize how wrong I've been. He told me that he did the same thing and it drove his wife away. They almost got a divorce. If it hadn't been for their pastor counseling them, they wouldn't have made it. Babe, I don't want to lose you ... will you please forgive me so that we can move forward?" Darren got on his knees, grabbed my hands and kissed them. He was crying. I could see the pain and hurt in his eyes. It never dawned on me that Darren was hurting too and that made my heart melt.

"Baby, I feel so foolish and I'm sorry too. I love you, Darren," I said, sobbing like I was at a funeral.

I had everything that I needed in Darren and I can't believe I was willing to throw it all away. Darren has always been good to me and my kids; he genuinely cared about me.

"Babe, I want to talk to you about the girls," Darren said.

"I'm sorry about the

things I've said about them and I'll try really hard to have a better relationship with them."

"I'm glad to hear you say that because they'll be here permanently," Darren said slowly.

"*Permanently*? And just when had you planned on telling me? Oh *now* I see. You apologize to me, get me feeling all mushy and then make a decision without consulting me. You even had nerve enough to cry. Wow, Darren, just … *wow*. This is un-*freaking*-believable. What's next? Will Mother Holley be moving in too?" I asked, sarcastically. "Darren, you get the actor of the year award for real!" I yelled.

"Angelia, the girls are here for a good reason," Darren said calmly.

"Okay, let me guess: Marcy ran away and joined the circus … oh no, I got it. She joined the Army.

"Angelia, STOP IT! That's enough!" Darren looked up to make sure the kids weren't approaching the room.

"The girls are here because Elroy, Marcy's so-called boyfriend tried to force himself on Skylar. Tyler walked in on him and ran to the neighbor's house to get help. Elroy has been touching her inappropriately for quite some time, apparently, and this time he tried to take it a step further," Darren said with a shaky voice.

I was in shock. I dropped my head and cried. All I could think about was what Sheila said about the girls needing love. Skylar wasn't the best kid in the world, but she certainly didn't deserve this.

"Where are the kids now?" I asked.

"They're all upstairs in Amber's room watching a movie."

"What did Marcy say? Did the police pick him up?"

"Yes, the police picked him up and he better be glad that they arrived before I did. I would've killed him for messing with my baby. Oh God ... my baby needed me and I failed her. I couldn't protect her, Angelia, I couldn't protect her," Darren cried.

I held him in my arms. I'd never seen my husband like this before. I couldn't find any words to say. I realized that with everything that's been going on, we hadn't been this close in quite a while. We hadn't been intimate in two weeks. I held him tighter and we both sat there crying and rocking each other. I was so used to Darren being the strong one. Sheila was right, I wanted a change. A change in my marriage, a change in my life, a change within our family.

Maybe we all needed to go to church. So much had happened within the last few months ... It couldn't hurt. Even Amber said she wished we could go every Sunday. At that moment I realized that my husband was going to need me in the months to come. *I have no idea what to do or how I'm going to do it, but no matter what, we're going to get through this.*

I closed my eyes and silently prayed and asked God to give me strength to help my husband through this storm. For the first time in years I felt like God actually heard my prayer. I don't know if I was delusional or what, but I heard a voice telling me, *Let go and trust*

Me. I suddenly felt a sense of peace … like God was right there with me. I cried even harder and so did Darren; we both cried and continued holding one another in silence.

Chapter 14

"Honey, we're going to get through this," I said, lifting Darren's face up so that he could see me.

"I just don't know where I went wrong, Angelia." Darren blamed himself.

"You didn't do anything wrong, and I will not let you take the blame for what that monster, Elroy did. The girls were in Marcy's custody when this happened and although they were in her care, it's not her fault either. Help me get upstairs so that I can check on the kids. When I left here they all looked scared, so I want to reassure them that everything is okay."

I grabbed my crutches and Darren and I hobbled along until we finally made it to the top of the stairs. I didn't know what to expect, so I took a deep breath and knocked on Amber's door and went in.

"Mom, you're back." Amber jumped up and hugged me.

"Yeah, Mom we were scared something bad happened to you," Demarcus said and hugged me too.

"I'm fine, I just sprained my ankle. It should be better in a few days."

Both Tyler and Skylar sat in silence—which was a first. Skylar looked as if she was in a daze.

"It's getting late. You guys should all prepare for bed; it's been a long day," Darren said.

"Skylar, please follow us to our bedroom," I said.

I wanted to make sure that Skylar was okay; she looked so

scared and confused. I had to find a way to let her know that I was there for her.

Darren, Skylar and I went into our bedroom and Skylar sat in my navy blue chaise chair in the far corner of the room.

"Skylar, please come sit next to me," I said to her, a deliberate smile in place.

Skylar looked confused, as if she couldn't believe I was asking her to sit close to me. Rightfully so, since I had acted such a nut with her in previous encounters.

"It's okay, Skylar," Darren said and smiled at her.

Skylar came over and sat on the bed next to me, but not too close; she still wasn't convinced that it was safe.

"Skylar, I want you to know what happened to you tonight isn't your fault. I am sure that Elroy probably told you that this is normal and that if you didn't go along with what he asked of you, he would kill you and your family."

"How did you know, Ms. Angelia?"

"I know because when I was your age, my best friend's dad tried to do the same thing to me. Sabrina and I were the best of friends and I used to spend the night at her house. One night I woke up because I heard a noise; Sabrina's dad was in her room. He came over to the bed and tried to kiss me. He held me down and when I tried to get up, he wouldn't let me go. I kicked and scratched him and we woke Sabrina and that made him stop. I ran out of the house and down the street and called my mom to come and get me.

"The difference between you and me is that my mother

didn't call the police. I was no longer allowed to go to Sabrina's house. Years later we found out that Sabrina's dad was molesting her. I'm so glad that Tyler was able to get help when she did."

"I was so scared, he was holding me down and he tried to … he tried to …." Skylar was so overwhelmed with tears that she couldn't finish the sentence. She was shaking uncontrollably.

"Shhhhhh. It's okay, baby, we're here for you. Your dad and I are here and we're going to get through this," I said, pulling Skylar into my arms and rocking her.

"Angelia is right, Skylar, we are here and we're going to get through this. I'm going to make sure that Elroy pays for what he tried to do to you."

"Daddy, I don't ever want to go back there again."

"Don't worry, sweetheart, you won't ever have to go back there again," I said. Darren looked at me and smiled. I could tell he had a sense of relief.

"Ms. Angelia, thanks for letting me stay here," Skylar said.

"This is your home too; we're family. Your dad and I will have to get with Marcy so that we can get you and Tyler enrolled in school. You have nothing to worry about; everything's going to be okay."

"Alright, pumpkin, let's get you to bed," Darren said.

"Goodnight, Skylar."

"Goodnight, Ms. Angelia," Skylar said, and gave me a hug. Darren joined in before leaving the room.

Darren walked Skylar to

her bedroom and my head was spinning like crazy. I was going from two kids to four kids. I didn't know how I was going to do it, but I was going to make a difference in those girls' lives. They needed me.

"Angelia, baby, thank you for being there for Skylar. Words can't express how grateful I am to have you."

"Darren, it's like you said, you accepted Amber and Demarcus so it's only right for me to do the same with Tyler and Skylar."

"You are amazing," Darren said, and leaned in and kissed me.

It truly felt good to be kissing him again. I didn't realize how much I really missed Darren, his hugs, his kisses, sharing a bed with him. Most of the time when Darren made it home extremely late, he would just sleep in one of the guest bedrooms. Tonight I was going to enjoy this moment of being with my husband in every way. Darren kissed me hungrily and we allowed that kiss to take us to what we both had been missing, what we both needed.

I rolled over and looked at the clock and saw it was 9:30 a.m. I hadn't planned on sleeping that long and I'm sure the pain medication played a role in it too. I tried to get out of bed and then remembered that my ankle was sprained. I guess after having such an intense night with Darren I forgot about my injury. I needed to get up and go check on the children. I rolled over and looked on the nightstand for my cell phone but then remembered that we had an intercom. I called into the den where I knew the kids would be.

"Hello, is anybody there?" I called.

"Babe, do you need something?" Darren answered.

"Ummmmmmm, what are you doing home? I figured you would be at work."

"I called Coach Minden and he insisted that I stay home after I told him what was going on. I'm coming upstairs, be there in a few, okay?"

"Okay," I said, with a huge smile on my face.

I couldn't believe that Darren was actually going to be at home today, especially since the first game of the season is this coming Friday.

"Angelia, babe, how is your ankle?"

"It feels okay. I think I need to try to start walking on it."

"You've got to take it easy, babe. Give it another day or so. Honey, Marcy is on her way over here to bring the girls' clothes and for us to sit down and talk."

"Yes, I agree we need to talk. Help me get up and get showered so that I'll be ready when she arrives."

Marcy arrived about an hour later looking like warmed over death. I could look at her and tell that she hadn't had any sleep. Poor thing looked a wreck: her hair hadn't been combed, she didn't have on any makeup and her clothes were mismatched. I'd never seen her look like this before. I could only imagine what she must be going through. I am sure that if it was Amber, I would have been the same way.

"Marcy, I want to thank you for agreeing to let me have custody of the girls," Darren said.

"It's temporary, Darren, I'm not letting you take my kids."

"I'm not taking them; I just want the girls to be in a safe, stable environment."

"Are you saying it's my fault that this happened?" Marcy asked.

"Nobody is accusing you of anything; this is Elroy's fault," I chimed in.

"This has nothing to do with you, Ms. Goody Goody," Marcy lashed out at me.

"That's where you're wrong. This has everything to do with Angelia. Angelia will be the one taking care of the girls while I'm at football practice. I'll be here, true enough, but she'll be with them the majority of the time. Angelia is their stepmother and whether you accept that or not is really irrelevant."

I had never heard Darren speak to Marcy like that but was glad that he finally put her in her rightful place.

"Look Marcy, we're both adults, and I am here to help. Your girls are important to me as well," I said.

"Since when?" Marcy asked with an attitude.

"Since right now. What happened in the past shouldn't have happened; we've both said some things that we shouldn't have said. Let's start over for the sake of the girls," I said, reaching out to hug her, and to my surprise she hugged me back.

"Alright, but I want to be able to see my babies when I want to," Marcy said.

"You can come and see the girls anytime … all I ask is that you call first. I need their birth certificates so that I can enroll them at Lancing Springs Intermediate," Darren said.

"I have their birth certificates and shot records with me now. Angelia, take care of my babies." Marcy turned to me with tears in her eyes.

"I'll take care of them as if they were my own," I said, and I really meant it.

Chapter 15

The Lancing Springs High School band had the stands
rocking with a feisty rendition of Michael Jackson's "Bad."
The drill team's throwback dance included the Moonwalk,
which probably shouldn't have been performed on turf with
white dance boots. But they tried it, and the crowd went wild as
they performed during the half-time show.

The score was tied 7-7 before the break, both teams having
scored touchdowns from interceptions. My husband was
completely enthralled with the game. From the 50-yardline
seats reserved for coaches' families, I watched along with
Amber, Demarcus, Skylar and Tyler, and a horde of supporters
who hoped that all of their two-a-day practicing would pay off
in a winning season. I joked with Coach Minden's wife that we
weren't giving up our husbands for nothing—we wanted a
championship!

While the kids and families were into the game, I couldn't
take my eyes off of Darren. *Dang, he looks good.* With his
headphones in place, chewing that gum, commanding those
boys like an Army sergeant, my husband could have been
starring in a major motion picture. For the first time in a long
time, I noticed his biceps bulging in his form-fitting Lancing
Tigers shirt, his powerful thighs peeking out of the bottom of
his khaki shorts.

My grandmother used to say that the Lord didn't involve
Himself in sports, but I prayed that they would win anyway

because I wanted to give my husband a private congratulatory party.

The smile on my face sharply broke when Demarcus brushed up against my foot, which I had resting on the seat in front of me. "Be careful!" I fussed as a reflex.

He slowed to a snail's pace as he crossed in front of my leg holding the drink and chips he and Tyler had just purchased from the concession stand.

"Boy, say you're sorry," she ordered.

"Sorry," he snapped at her.

She mean-mugged him. "You'd better not hit your Momma's foot again."

Tyler carefully passed my leg, then took her seat between Demarcus and Skylar. Seconds later, he asked if he could have one of her nachos.

"Just one." She watched as he withdrew a single tortilla chip.

"Thank you."

"Don't let the cheese spill on your shirt."

In the past week, since the girls moved in, it had become increasingly clear to me that Demarcus had a love-hate relationship with his stepsisters, especially Tyler. They argued, but he'd ask her to play outside with him before he'd ask Amber. And more often than not, Tyler would join him.

The more I sat back and observed their interactions through a lens of love rather than annoyance, I realized that Tyler was quite the protective, helpful mother hen. A bit overbearing, but she meant well—even when she popped Demarcus on the back of his neck for playing with my crutches.

I imagined that she and Skylar had a long talk and decided that I wasn't the wicked witch of the west. Or maybe Marcy had something to do with their change of heart. Either way, this truce showed me that even when Tyler was in a good mood, she had a blunt personality that could easily be mistaken for rudeness. She said what she meant and meant what she said. Had she been too thoroughly trained in being proper, suppressing her feelings, and biting her tongue, she might not have spoken up about Elroy.

Sheila was right. Tyler just needed to be trained in how to use her powers for good.

At the moment, she was using that loud mouth of hers to scream for the Tigers' lead running back, K.J. Mc Daniels. "Gooooo K-J! Gooooooo!"

Everyone in our section jumped to their feet, which completely blinded my view of the field.

Well, almost everyone. I looked down my row and saw Amber still seated, texting on her phone. I cupped my mouth so my voice would travel over the screaming. "Hey!"

Amber looked my way. She gave me a thumbs-up and a forced smile.

I gave her my thumbs-up, too, wondering what was on my daughter's mind, why she was wearing such a fake grin.

Of course, a football game wasn't the place to have a heart-to-heart.

K.J.'s run came to an end after a 17-yard gain and the crowd returned to a sitting position. I tried to catch Amber's eye again to ask her to sit on my right side, which was empty, but she either didn't see me or was ignoring me.

What's wrong with her? I mentally replayed all that had happened since we moved into the house. Suddenly, she had two sisters, a new school, more housework to help me with— and I really couldn't even help in my condition.

Maybe we should get a housekeeper for the next few weeks. Amber needed a break. She might even need to go back to Dallas for a few days over Thanksgiving break or go to Marshall and spend some time with her paternal grandmother. Get reconnected with her old friends. Be a kid for these last few months before college, not that she had ever had a real childhood.

When K.J. ran in for the touchdown, Amber stood with the rest of the crowd. I knew then that she was avoiding me because my baby girl couldn't care less about a football game.

I made a mental note to schedule some mother-daughter time with Amber. And that's when it hit me: All this time I'd been complaining about Darren not being there for me, and I hadn't been there for Amber. *Ain't that the pot calling the kettle black?*

K.J. ran for two more touchdowns in the third quarter, sealing a win early for our team. Nonetheless, my husband continued to coach like they were in the first quarter. "Don't let up!" I heard him tell a huddle of boys. "You don't go easy when you're ahead. Stick to   the grind. Got it?"

131

"Yes, coach!" they said together.

"You guys are the best. Don't ever let anyone tell you otherwise. You're the *best* athletes, the *best* students, with the *most* heart!"

Watching him and hearing him speak such encouraging words to those eager sets of eyes staring back through the helmet bars nearly made me tear up.

Mrs. Minden tapped me on the shoulder. "You must be very proud of your husband."

"I am."

"You should be. What he's doing is more than coaching. It's a calling. A ministry. He'll do well here at Lancing Springs."

"Thank you."

She quickly turned her attention back to the field, yelling as the Tigers scored yet another touchdown.

"Momma." Demarcus approached me with papers in hand, the twins following behind him.

I stirred the ground turkey in the skillet a few times, then rested my wooden spoon on the rim. I could hardly wait for school to start the following week. Cooking for five during the week was no joke, especially since I had to sit on a stool to slave over the stove.

"What's up?"

"Me, Tyler and Skylar—"

"Tyler, Skylar and *I*," I corrected him.

"Yes. Us."

Skylar covered her mouth to keep from laughing.

"Proceed," I said.

"We got a plan for fixing the star in the foyer. We can start on it today."

I raised an eyebrow. "Okay, the people who built this house say they can't fix it for weeks, until they get a certain wood in stock. They may even have to put in a whole new star. How do you three plan to repair it *today*?"

Tyler took the papers from him and pushed him away with her hip.

"Stop!" he protested, repositioning himself right at her side.

"So." She sprawled the papers on the counter as I resumed stirring the meat for our turkey tacos. "We can take out the wooden triangles in the five stars. We can replace them with colorful tiles."

Skylar added, "Like a mosaic."

I studied the pictures. Honestly, they didn't look half-bad. A nice splash of color in the star might add some character to the design. Make it our own.

"We set the glass pieces in place with this grout stuff for floors. Then we paint over it with a clear coating to set it in place. And we've got a new star instead of it looking like somebody carved a hole in our entryway."

"Yeah. It *was* y'all's fault," Demarcus teased.

"Whatever," from the girls.

"So can we do it?" Skylar

practically begged. "Please, please, please? I mean, it's gonna be even better than it was before."

"Yeah, 'cause we're gonna, like, blend all these colors together instead of having just one boring brown star." Tyler animated her words with swooping hand gestures.

I put a hand to my hip. "What if y'all mess up my floor?"

"It's *already* messed up!" Skylar said.

She definitely spoke the truth. That star was jacked.

"And if we mess up, they can just go ahead and replace the whole star anyway. But at least we tried, right?"

"So can we do it, Ma? It's worth a try." Demarcus pled their case.

All three pressed their hands together as though praying. Their eager faces made me laugh. "Okay, so long as—"

"Yes!" They hi-fived each other before I could even voice the condition that they made sure to clean up their mess each night.

They rushed through dinner and helped Amber clean up quickly so we could make a trip to Home Depot. Amber said she didn't want to go with us. Instead, she was going to help Miss Earlene bake cookies for a daycare center.

How could I say no to that?

The younger kids and I spent a good hour in that store as a very capable associate examined the kids' printouts and the current pictures of our floor they'd captured on Tyler's phone. The helpful worker talked us through what we'd need and answered questions until the kids and I felt confident they could get the job done.

We purchased the supplies, went back home, and I just let them have at it. Honestly, I was glad to have them doing something productive, not arguing, and out of my hair for a few hours each day that week.

One day, I stood above them and took a picture of the three of them sprawled out on the floor together working on the star, surrounded by hundreds of brightly colored tiles, a bucket of grout, and their putty knives. The mother's heart in me ached for Marcy. She was missing out on these girls. Missing out on projects, this learning experience, the daily joy of watching your kids do things you never even knew they could do.

I decided to send the photo to Marcy via text.

She replied: *You don't know how good you have it. Kiss my girls goodnight for me.*

I said: *I certainly will. Night.*

Night.

Chapter 16

"What a friend we have in Jesus," the congregation of Mighty Movement of God Worship Center sang in unison. I was thankful they were singing something I recognized from the weekends I'd spent in church with my grandmother.

This small church, with three sections of pews, the pulpit, and a traditional choir stand behind the pulpit, could have just as well been the one in Marshall. The wooden church attendance board with black-and-white tiles displayed the number in attendance last week and the amount of offering, 169 and $531 respectively.

I heard Darren, standing to my left, keeping up with the words. "Oh, what peace we often forfeit ..."

But as I glanced at all four of the kids to my right and saw them all fumbling through the simple lines, I felt convicted. These kids knew all the words to the latest rap songs, but probably didn't know one hymn or even a scripture that might comfort them during a tough season.

Skylar, especially, needed to know something about God. Her counseling sessions had exposed a lot of underlying anxiety. Having Tyler for a twin had been Skylar's saving grace thus far. There would come a day, however, when Skylar would need to stand on her own two feet and learn her own strength. If she had God in her corner, she'd be much better off.

After our time of singing, the church secretary approached the standing microphone, adjusted her feathered hat, and asked the visitors to stand and introduce ourselves. Turned out, half of those in attendance were there for Friends & Family day. Those seated applauded us for coming.

I poked Darren and whispered, "You got us?"

"Yeah." When it was our turn, my husband did the honors, introducing us from left to right. "My name is Darren Holley. This is my wife, Angelia. Our son Demarcus. Daughters Skylar, Tyler, and Amber. We're guests of Miss Earlene and Sister Sheila."

Sheila waved from the choir stand, Miss Earlene from the front pew.

One of the deacons shouted, "He's the new coach at the high school, y'all," which brought another round of applause.

The secretary nodded. "We're glad to have you all with us. What a good-looking family. But now, if you're going to represent Mighty Movement of God, we need a better record this season."

My husband smiled and graciously tipped his head to her.

I was so proud of him. So proud of our family as we stood there in color-coordinated outfits. I wished I could run up to that microphone and tell everyone in the church our story—how this was my third marriage and Darren's second, and how our family was in such a terrible place only a few weeks earlier, but thanks to some divine intervention, we were standing there as a rock-solid unit.

The secretary moved on to the next group of visitors, so we sat. Darren squeezed my hand. I squeezed his back.

The choir sang a song.

Then we gave in the offering. Following that blessing, one of the members of the pulpit announced that it was prayer time and the altar was open for anyone who wanted prayer.

To my surprise, Amber scurried past those at the end of our row and made her way to the front of the church. Darren looked at me with a question mark in his eyes. I shrugged, then returned my gaze to the front. From behind, I could see my daughter's shoulders shaking. She was heaving as she cried.

I made a beeline to the altar and met up with my daughter, as did Miss Earlene. Amber sobbed, her hands covering her face. My mothering instincts knew something was terribly wrong. Maybe something so wrong that only the Lord could fix it. I wanted to hug her, tell her everything would be okay, but would it?

Miss Earlene grabbed my hand and placed it on Amber's back, as though she knew I needed guidance in this situation. I began to rub my daughter's shoulders even as I searched Miss Earlene's face for answers. Miss Earlene rolled her lips between her teeth and gave me a slow nod. It struck me that my neighbor obviously knew more about my daughter than I did.

This was brand new territory for me. I'd been a mother since I was nineteen, but my own mother passed before I reached Amber's age. Somehow, I guess I thought Amber was self-sufficient because I was forced to be self-sufficient before I finished high school. Apparently, this wasn't the truth.

"Ohhhh, ohhh my brother, pray for me," the church continued to sing as more people ambled toward the altar.

Miss Earlene whispered into Amber's ear.

My daughter wiped her eyes briefly, though tears continued to flow. She looked at me and said, through trembling lips, the words no mother of a high school age daughter ever wants to hear. "Mom. I'm pregnant."

My mouth dropped open. *Amber? My sweet, quiet daughter?* "Honey…what? What are you saying? Wh … who?"

Miss Earlene pulled us into a tight circle. "We can get to the bottom of this a little later—"

"Why didn't you tell me?"

"I tried, but you were always—"

"And you chose to tell me *now*? *Here*?"

Miss Earlene intervened, "What better place to confess than at the altar?"

I sighed, feeling as though my heart had dropped to the bottom of my stomach. *My daughter? A-student—Pregnant?* I could almost hear the sound of her promising future swooshing down a toilet, the same way mine had been swept away when I got pregnant with her.

The thought of my baby living a lifetime of hardship brought a lump to my throat. *This is so not what I wanted for her.*

"When you bow, at the altar…" belted around me.

Me? A grandmother! Not a step-grandmother, a REAL grandmother. *I'm not even forty years old yet! How embarrassing.*

Amber hung her head as the preacher prayed for all of us gathered in a semi-circle at the feet of the Lord.

I bowed my head, too, because this was too much.

Again, Miss Earlene guided my hand to comfort my daughter as we both wept.

I'm not sure what the minister prayed, but I said "Amen" with everyone else and followed Amber back to our row. Lord knows I wanted to go outside and talk to her, but I was still in shock.

"Everything okay?" Darren asked.

"No."

He waited for elaboration.

I couldn't even speak the words from my mouth. "I'll tell you later."

Out of the corner of my eye, I could see Amber wiping tears from her face and Tyler hugging her big sister. *Do the twins know already?*

Shoot, the whole world might know already.

My eyes wouldn't stay dry during the choir's second song, "If You're Happy, Say Amen."

I was anything but happy, which caught Darren's attention. He leaned down. "Babe. Do we need to go outside and talk?"

"No. It's … the beautiful song."

He snapped, "Stop lying in church. This is a happy song, but you're crying. What's wrong?"

"Amber's pregnant," I hissed back at him.

His eyes grew wide. "What? When?"

"I don't know."

"Who is the knucklehead?"

"I said I don't know."

My husband crossed his arms. "I need to know what's going on."

"Join the club."

The pastor took the podium and prayed before his sermon. My body was present, but my mind was racing in circles. *When did Amber have time to sleep with someone? Was it a boy from Marshall? Dallas?* I hoped to God it wasn't anyone from Lancing Springs because we'd just moved there. If she was hopping in bed with boys she just met, my child was *out there* and I hadn't even known.

Then horror struck as I wondered if Amber had been raped or if she was involved with an older man who was manipulating her. *Should we call the police?* We were already about to be involved with the courts regarding Skylar. One more case was fine with me.

I calmed myself down with a bit of self-talk. *Stop torturing yourself. Amber is not a sex slave. If she's figured out that she's pregnant, it must be from a boy back home because she hasn't been in Lancing Springs long enough to be one hundred percent certain.*

I began to recall the times Amber had come to my room wanting to talk in private, but I'd shooed her away. And she kept herself holed up in her bedroom, though I figured it was just the stress of moving away from familiar surroundings and transferring to a new school her senior year. All along, she'd needed me to be a mother to her. *My poor baby.*

When the pastor finished

praying, he said, "I know you all smell the food coming from the fellowship hall. Sister Winan is throwing down, and I know you want to get to it, so I won't be before you long."

The audience laughed.

Then he announced, in a way that made me feel as though he was talking directly to me, "There *is* a word from the Lord."

My mind stilled for a moment.

"For the purpose of speaking directly to our friends and family who may not be as familiar with all the scriptures, I'm not going to use a bunch of thees and thous. Amen?"

The body agreed.

"So I'm going to read James chapter one, verses two through four from The Message Bible. It reads as such: Consider it a sheer gift, friends, when tests and challenges come at you from all sides. You know that under pressure, your faith-life is forced into the open and shows its true colors. So don't try to get out of anything prematurely. Let it do its work so you become mature and well-developed, not deficient in any way."

"Mmm hmmm," from the audience.

"Yes sir!" from the deacon who liked to add extra commentary.

"I believe the Lord is encouraging us through these scriptures specifically. I don't know about you, but sometimes it feels like fifteen problems are hitting me at once."

"Amen," flew out of my mouth.

"And just when you get one solved, here comes another

one. Bigger. Worse."

My body rocked in agreement. This man was preaching straight to my soul. "No matter what you're going through, God isn't the author of the problems. But He is the author of our faith. The problems and hardships He allows aren't to tear us down. They're to build our dependence on Him."

Darren said "Amen" this time as he laced his fingers with mine.

"The Bible promises that the end result is spiritual maturity, development, and the peace of knowing that you are whole in Him come hell or high water."

As the preacher expounded on the message, Darren and I somehow ended up scooting toward each other. My tears continued to flow, but these were not as bitter as the ones I'd shed at the altar only a few minutes earlier. These scriptures, which seemed almost a force of life within themselves, had breathed new hope into my heart.

We could handle the twins. The new baby. The house. Even staying married through football season—if we kept our eyes on God.

Following the sermon, when the pastor asked for people who wanted to accept Christ or join the church, Darren and I both stood simultaneously. To the audience, it might have looked as though we'd planned to stand together, but we hadn't.

It was the Lord.

Darren looked down our row, tilted his head to the left. Our kids stood and followed us to the altar, where my husband and I rededicated our lives to the Lord. Darren told the pastor we were joining the church.

As an afterthought, while the pastor spoke briefly with the other people who had come to the altar, Darren asked softly, "Umm…you cool with this?"

I nearly laughed. "Are you kidding me? We won't make it without Him."

He kissed my temple. "But we can win. Together."

"Together. In Him," I agreed.

With our new pastor standing in front of us and the church's prayers behind us, we became members of Mighty Movement of God Worship Center.

Standing there at the altar that morning, Darren and I were oblivious to all the challenges that lay ahead of us as a blended family. But we were confident that whatever came at us— babies, exes, in-laws, grandchild-baby-daddy-issues, court cases, cracked floors—whatever! With the help of the Lord, our unique family would always be a blessing.

~The End~

A Sneak Peak at

Through it All

Book 2 of the Blended Blessings Series

Since that Sunday five months earlier, our family had been attending service regularly. The members called us by my husband's last name—the Holley's. Amber was the "oldest Holley girl", then the "twin Holley girls", the "Holley boy" was Demarcus. I became "Sister Holley" and they called my husband "Coach Holley" because he coached for the Lancing Springs High School varsity football team. Even though Amber's real last name was Norrel and Demarcus's last name was Jackson—from my two previous marriages—I think my kids liked carrying Darren's last name in our church family. Darren and I didn't correct people about the last names, either, because I didn't want people all in my business with my third marriage.

Unfortunately, Amber's pregnancy put our family business front and center. Every time I looked at her baby bump, I could hardly believe that was *my* daughter looking like a single-parent-reared African-American statistic.

The next thing I wondered was where I went wrong. Did I not pay her enough attention? Did I not supervise her enough?

She didn't even get to take off her church clothes that day before I lit into her. I followed her straight to her bedroom when we got home because I had a laundry list of questions.

"First of all, since *when* did you become sexually active?"

She sat still and kept her eyes on the woven tan carpet in her room while I paced around her bed like a shark about to take a bite out of her behind. Only I couldn't because she was carrying my grandchild.

Grandchild.

"Answer me!"

"It was only one time," she squeaked.

"That's all it *takes* is one time!"

"I know. We tried to use protection, but—"

"But what?!"

She sighed, "It didn't work."

I tried to picture exactly how the protection didn't work, but the mental image of my daughter laid up in bed with a boy was too ridiculous to visualize. "Obviously it didn't work! And who is the boy?"

"J. D."

I stopped at the foot her bed. "Who in the world is J. D? I've never even heard you speak his name and now he's the father of my grandchild."

"Jake Durham. He's from my old school. In Dallas. We had some classes together. Electives."

Since Amber was enrolled in all advanced courses, I took her response to mean that he wasn't in the advanced diploma program. Anger, embarrassment, and frustration got the best of me as I asked, "So, he's stupid?"

"No, he's not stupid." She flipped her hair behind over her

shoulder and finally looked up at me. "He's smart. Just not book-smart."

Her eyes carried the slight glimmer of a school-girl's crush. I realized then that my daughter actually had feelings for J.D. Part of me was glad to know that she hadn't jumped in bed for a one-night stand. But another part of me knew that Amber was probably headed for her first heartbreak. And this one would be a doozy because she'd be left with a baby.

I sat on the bed beside her. "Amber, honey. Are you and Jake still in a relationship?"

"It's kind of hard to be together when we're so far apart," she said.

"Well, do you talk to him? Text him?"

"Sometimes. He's really busy. He works a lot."

"Where does he work?"

"Jack-in-the-box. He's a shift manager."

"How is he working as a manager and going to school, too?"

She hesitated. "He's not in school anymore. He dropped out."

My hand flew to my forehead. *Oh, Lord! I knew he was stupid!*

"But he's going to get his G-E-D," my daughter had tried to clean it up.

From then on, I had no hope for this child's father. Granted, getting a G-E-D is not the worst thing that could happen to a person. My cousin Thomasina got her G-E-D and went on to open a successful medical transcription service. But Thomasina had issues that prevented her from finishing high school under normal circumstances.

I suspected Jake had issues, too. He didn't know how to "work" birth control. He'd dropped out of school, and he couldn't sustain a long-distance relationship despite all the technology available these days.

"Momma, I'm sorry. I didn't mean for this to happen."

"Don't be sorry to me. This is *your* life you just threw a monkey-wrench in."

"I know. But I've already started looking at social services. I can get on Medicaid and get help with childcare."

I shook my head. "Really, Amber? You think the fact that you're getting on welfare makes everything better?"

"No. But I'm trying."

I'd heard enough. I had left her room that evening wondering what, other than a crush, had gotten hold of her. Why would a young lady with colleges knocking on her door, with her whole future ahead of her, risk everything for one moment with a drop-out Jack-in-the-Box manager?

I didn't even make it back to my bedroom before the answer to that question hit me.

She learned it from me.

In all my years as a single mother, Amber had watched the kind of men I dated before I met Darren. With few exceptions, I loved me a thug. A womanizing, street-smart thug just like her father, who was serving a life sentence for attempted capital murder.

That night, I had cried a river down Darren's chest, telling him how Amber's pregnancy was all my fault. I should have been a better model, a better mother.

"Baby, Amber made her own choices," he tried to comfort me.

It was no use. Though I was never one to bring men home to my kids, I couldn't deny the example I had set for her, kissing all those frogs before I finally met my prince.

Once I accepted my part in this whole fiasco, I think my attitude actually got better. As weird as it sounded, I somehow, I felt better once I put some of the blame on myself. I was able to jump in the boat with my daughter and stop crying over what had already been done.

The baby was growing inside her belly and I was going to be a grandmother soon whether I liked it or not. I could be mad and neglect my daughter again or get over myself and be there for her. With the help of the Lord through teachings at my church and sharing my pain with the women in our small group, I realized that I wasn't the first woman to go through this, nor would I be the last.

By the time the New Year rolled around, I was all-in, planning to help Amber any way that I could. The first step was setting up the baby shower.

Of course, we'd invite Jake and his family. But I wasn't quite ready for the new kind of special they brought to the table.

Through it All
Coming Spring, 2015!

Possible Discussion Questions

1. Why do you think Angelia was so willing to secretly meet up with Sherman?

2. Do you think Mother Holley and Angelia will ever be friends? Have you ever had a Mother Holley in your life? If so, how did you handle the situation?

3. Angelia basically worshipped her house. Has there ever been a time in your life when you've put material things before God?

4. Angelia lives in fear that the good times in her life won't last long. Have you ever felt this way? What does the Bible say about fear and about what He gives us new each day?

5. Would you consider Miss Earlene a nosey neighbor or was she a big help to the Holley family?

6. Do you think Marcy was jealous of the life Angelia and Darren had?

7. Do you think Sheila was right for intervening in Angelia's situation?

8. Angelia seems to think that Amber, age 17, doesn't need her anymore. Do you think this may be related to the fact that Angelia didn't have a mother when she was Amber's age? How can parents learn to do for their children what wasn't done for them?

9. Do you feel Darren was right for taking the kids from Marcy?

10. Angelia feels overwhelmingly embarrassed when she learns that Amber is pregnant. How much of your children's actions are simply a result of their individual choices rather than poor upbringing?

11. Darren, Angelia, and even Sherman all say that their first marriages were mistakes because they were young and clueless. Is "we were young and clueless" a valid reason to end a marriage?

About the Authors

CaSandra McLaughlin was raised in Marshall, Texas. Growing up she wrote poems and loved to read books. She remembers being excited every time the book mobile came to her school. Reading always took her to another place, and often she would find herself rewriting an author's story. CaSandra wrote a play in high school for theatre that she received a superior rating on, and from there she aspired to be a writer.

CaSandra's a true believer that God has blessed us all with gifts and talents and it's up to us to tap into them to make our dreams come true. She's always dreamed of being on radio, TV and being an author. CaSandra currently works for a Gospel radio station and now she's an author. That lets her know that dreams come true—two down and one more to go. CaSandra wants people to read her work and feel encouraged, and it's her prayer that they read something that will change their lives and give them a ray of hope that things will be better. She's praying that God will continue to use her to write novels with several life lessons to help inspire the world.

CaSandra currently lives in Glenn Heights, Texas with her husband Richard and they have two amazing children. CaSandra loves God, her family, church, her friends, reading and Mexican food, in that order. Peace and blessings to all. Thanks for the love and support.

Visit CaSandra McLaughlin Online at
http://www.facebook.com/casandra.marshallmclaughlin

Michelle Stimpson

Michelle Stimpson's works include the highly acclaimed *Boaz Brown, Divas of Damascus Road* (National Bestseller), and *Falling Into Grace,* which has been optioned for a movie. She has published several short stories for high school students through her educational publishing company at WeGottaRead.com.

Michelle serves in women's ministry at her home church, Oak Cliff Bible Fellowship. She regularly speaks at special events and writing workshops sponsored by churches, schools, book clubs, and educational organizations.

The Stimpsons are proud parents of two young adults—one in college, one serving in the military—and one crazy dog.

Visit Michelle online:

www.MichelleStimpson.com

https://www.facebook.com/MichelleStimpsonWrites

Other Books by Michelle Stimpson

Fiction

A Forgotten Love (Novella) Book One in the "A Few Good Men" Series

The Start of a Good Thing (Novella) Book Two in the "A Few Good Men" Series

A Change of Heart (Novella) Book Three in the "A Few Good Men" SeriesA Shoulda Woulda Christmas (Novella)

Boaz Brown (Book 1 in the Boaz Brown Series)

No Weapon Formed (Book 2 in the Boaz Brown Series)

Divas of Damascus Road

Falling into Grace

I Met Him in the Ladies' Room (Novella)

I Met Him in the Ladies' Room Again (Novella)

Last Temptation (Starring "Peaches" from *Boaz Brown*)

Mama B: A Time to Speak (Book 1)

Mama B: A Time to Dance (Book 2)

Mama B: A Time to Love (Book 3)

Mama B: A Time to Mend (Book 4)

Someone to Watch Over Me

Stepping Down

The Good Stuff

Trouble In My Way (Young Adult)

What About Momma's House? (Novella with April Barker)

What About Love? (Novella with April Barker)

What About Tomorrow? (Novella with April Barker)

Non-Fiction

Did I Marry the Wrong Guy? And other silent ponderings of a fairly normal Christian wife

Uncommon Sense: 30 Truths to Radically Renew Your Mind in Christ

The 21-Day Publishing Plan

If you like this book, you'll want to read our literary friends! www.BlackChristianReads.com

Made in the USA
Middletown, DE
13 March 2020